TRANSLATED FROM THE
CATALAN BY MARUXA
RELAÑO AND MARTHA
TENNENT

GARDEN
BY
THE
SEA

Mercè
Rodoreda

OPEN LETTER
LITERARY TRANSLATIONS FROM THE UNIVERSITY OF ROCHESTER

Library of Congress Cataloging-in-Publication Data: Available
ISBN-13: 978-1-948830-08-9 | ISBN-10: 1-948830-08-6

*This project is supported in part by an award from the National Endowment for the Arts
and the New York State Council on the Arts with the support of
Governor Andrew M. Cuomo and the New York State Legislature.*

The translation of this work has been supported by the Institut Ramon Llull.

LLLL institut
ramon llull
Catalan Language and Culture

Text set in Fournier, a typeface designed by Pierre Simon Fournier (1712–1768),
a French punch-cutter, typefounder, and typographic theoretician.

Cover design by Alban Fischer
Interior design by Anthony Blake

Open Letter is the University of Rochester's nonprofit, literary translation press:
Dewey Hall 1-219, Box 278968, Rochester, NY 14627

www.openletterbooks.org

Praise for Mercè Rodoreda

"Rodoreda has bedazzled me by the sensuality with which she reveals things within the atmosphere of her novels."
—Gabriel García Márquez

"When you read [*Death in Spring*], read it for its beauty, for the way it will surprise and subvert your desires, and as a testament to the human spirit in the face of brutality and willful inhumanity."
—Jesmyn Ward, NPR

"It is a total mystery to me why Rodoreda isn't widely worshipped. . . . She's on my list of authors whose works I intend to have read all of before I die."
—John Darnielle, The Mountain Goats

"Mercè Rodoreda has been a favorite of mine ever since college. . . . *War, So Much War* helps to expand our understanding of a world-class writer's fiction, with hopefully more to come."
—Jeff VanderMeer

"Rodoreda plumbs a sadness that reaches beyond historic circumstances . . . an almost voluptuous vulnerability."
—Natasha Wimmer, *The Nation*

"Mercè Rodoreda is the writer I cannot stop talking about."
—Alberto Ríos

"The humor in the stories, as well as their thrill of realism, comes from a Nabokovian precision of observation and transformation of plain experience into enchanting prose."
—*Los Angeles Times*

ALSO BY
MERCÈ RODOREDA

A Broken Mirror
Camellia Street
Death in Spring
My Christina and Other Stories
The Selected Stories of Mercè Rodoreda
The Time of the Doves
War, So Much War

Dieu est au fond du jardin.

—Robert Kanters

GARDEN
BY
THE
SEA

I

I'VE ALWAYS ENJOYED KNOWING WHAT HAPPENS TO PEOPLE. It's not because I'm garrulous but because I like people, and I was fond of the owners of this house. But all of this happened so long ago that I can no longer recall many of the details. I'm old, and sometimes I get mixed up.

There was no need to go to the Excelsior to see films the summers they came with their friends. There was this one fellow who liked to paint the sea, Feliu Roca he was called. His work had been shown in exhibitions in Paris, and I believe he's known in Barcelona and made a pile of money with his swathes of blue. He had painted the sea in all of its incarnations: calm, wild, big waves, small waves. Green, the color of fear. Grey, the color of clouds. Seascapes. He said he did seascapes, and his friends encouraged him to dapple the canvas because that's what Americans like. They made fun of him and would say too many painters had painted the sea already; and then the young man, a good-looking fellow with ash blond hair and sleepy blue eyes . . . He stuttered sometimes. Such as when the colors didn't come out the way he wanted them. I'm referring to the paint mixture. And he would say to me: it's more difficult to paint this beast of blue than to tend flowers. And I would answer: you're right, yes you are. Flowers grow all by themselves. Maybe that's why there's so little merit in being a gardener. I said it just to make him happy, and he said when he finished painting the sea in every possible state of seaness, he would paint me, sitting in the sun. I didn't believe him. No. Every summer, when he came up, I was glad to see him again and I think he was glad to see me too. Six summers . . . all told, six summers and one terrible winter.

One of his female friends—there were two of them and they always came—was named Eulàlia. The other was Maragda. This Maragda was a seamstress and had been Senyoreta Rosamaria's boss when Rosamaria had worked for her as a young girl; that's how they became friends. When they returned from their morning swim, I always tried to busy myself with the nearby flowerbeds, the one that's full of marigolds in particular, so I could hear them talking. Such gaiety and youth, so much money . . . so much of everything . . . and two wrecked lives. I once saw a bird that let itself die. It must have been a desperate bird, desperate like Eugeni.

The first time I met the masters, the Senyorets, was in early spring, shortly after they were married. I knew the gentleman from before. I had seen him twice, once when he visited the estate with the intention of buying it, the other when he came to oversee the progress of the renovations. That second time he told me he would like me to stay, it suited him fine to keep me on as the gardener. They were to honeymoon abroad and were only stopping here for a short visit. Lots of strolls and time spent on the belvedere gazing at the ebb and flow of the waves, at the sky and all the movement within it, standing close to one another, sometimes holding each other. If ever I approached them during the day, I always coughed to make my presence known; it's no sin for a married couple to embrace, and yet I thought they wouldn't want to be seen. Quima, the cook, was already there that year. And after that they hired her every summer because the cook they had in Barcelona went home to her family. Quima made me tell her everything they did in the garden, and she told me everything that happened around the house. She got a lot of it from one of the maids, Miranda, a Brazilian girl. This Miranda wore a black dress, so formfitting on her snake-thin body that she would have been better off not wearing anything at all. And an apron of lace no larger than your hand. She thought she was something special. But there wasn't much for Quima to report because nothing much happened. Sometimes Senyoret Francesc would slip an olive into Senyoreta Rosamaria's mouth and she would take it with her little teeth. Apparently he was crazy about her. Quima said that when Miranda was telling her this, she, Miranda that is, who was the color of licorice, went pale. With envy, Quima said. These girls from Brazil are like that, it seems. One day they went out for a ride in the car and Quima took me upstairs. I was afraid they would come back and catch us. She said: "Wait till you see the jewelry she has! Senyoret Francesc is one of the wealthiest men in Barcelona!" And she showed me lots of baubles, all diamonds she said, and a necklace with a teardrop pendant dangling in the middle. Rich folks, they were, really rich. And trusting. Through the slats in the blinds we looked out at the garden. The grounds that came with the villa, and the adjacent lands, were fields of grass and weeds back then, teeming with lizards.

They left, saying they would be back in June with some friends. They handed me the keys and left me in charge of the house, which I was to air out from time to time. I was very pleased when I received the letter announcing their return. And just as they had instructed, I hired Quima for the summer, and her face flushed with delight because Senyoret Francesc mentioned in his letter that he especially liked her oven-baked sole. Miranda arrived with her huge suitcases two or three days before the rest of the family, and never opened her mouth. I headed outside to my plants. She, to the dust indoors. They came by sea. Three days later we heard a horn and I caught sight of the boat right away, coming in slowly, and when it was close enough they lowered the outboard. They stayed on the beach because they were already in their bathing costumes; they swam, and one of the friends began to skate on the water like a little figurine. They had brought an instructor to teach them, the skiing part I mean, and Senyoreta Rosamaria, just for laughs, asked me if I would like to learn myself, but I said my salad days were over. She asked if any of the flowers were ill, and I said I was glad to report they were all in fine health. They took on a new maid, Mariona, a village girl I knew by sight, very young, small and smooth as a pebble.

At night, from the mulberry and linden tree promenade, I would often find myself looking up at the masters' bedroom window. I have always enjoyed walking in the garden at night, to feel it breathe. And when I grew tired I would amble back to my little house, reveling in the peaceful existence of all that was green and filled with color in the light of day. Gradually I became aware that someone else was often in the garden at that late hour. I concealed myself and stood watch, and I saw it was Miranda. I was annoyed because she held a branch in her hand and was beating my plants with it as she walked. One night I came out of the shadows and gave her a piece of my mind.

"Miranda?" Quima said one day. "I don't like her. People who are awake during sleeping hours shouldn't be trusted. What Miranda is really after . . . but clearly Senyoret has eyes for only one thing. I don't think Senyoreta Rosamaria has any cause for concern."

"Some men are attracted to people from faraway places, so they can dream of exotic trees and colorful feathers," I said. "It suits them better." Quima said I was off my rocker and threatened never to speak to me again. I wasn't so crazy after all. Miranda played the innocent and went about laying her snares.

For a long time I knew very little about Senyoreta Eulàlia, the one who knew how to skate across the sea. Pale of skin and dark of hair, there was a reserved air about her. She was nothing like our Senyoreta, who radiated something that was like fair weather. For a while I suspected Feliu, the painter, was sweet on Eulàlia. But he was caught up in his painting. One day I teased him about it, and he said he wasn't attracted to ladies who put on airs, and the task of entertaining them should fall to someone else, and rather than a bouquet of roses he much preferred a bunch of . . . he pointed to some flowers. "Foxglove," I said. "A simple flower." And he said: "If I'm not careful, there are ladies who would devour me alive, and the painter would be finished before ever getting started."

I don't know if he was right, and he probably didn't either, but we both laughed. Now and again Quima would ask me what Miranda did at night.

"Nothing. She wanders about. As long as she doesn't harm my plants she can do as she pleases."

One moon-filled night she went for a swim. I wouldn't have recognized her if it hadn't been for the moon. She sprinted into the water as if entering a sea of ink. And when she emerged she gleamed like an olive. She stretched out on the sand and she lay there for so long I thought she had fallen asleep. And swoosh, swoosh, swoosh went the water, here I come and there I go. I mimicked the frog's call and Miranda didn't move. Still as death. I finally tired of singing and went home to bed. And just as I was falling asleep: croak, croak, croak beneath my window. I could have strangled her. I pretended to be asleep and I have resented her ever since.

One day Senyoreta came to see the garden and I showed her the nursery. "These tiny ones here? They'll turn into flowers," I said. "By the time you leave they will have bloomed and nothing will be left of them, only the seeds." She seemed taken aback, apparently no one had ever made it plain to her what happens to all those little plants that are grown from seeds. I took a good look at her: she was pretty. There was something about her that I, the gardener that I am, wouldn't know how to explain, because I have a hard time describing delicate things. And even if gardeners are different from most people, and this comes from working with flowers, we also work with the earth. You might say one thing balances the other. But when it comes to her, Senyoreta I mean, it was all flowers. I think I'm getting tangled up now. I liked Senyoreta a lot, to look at I mean. Sometimes I wanted to say to her: "Sit. Please sit down so I can look at you." Naturally, I never dared to. But I might have if I hadn't believed that, on top of thinking I was mad, she might let me go.

"Lived here long?" Feliu asked one day as he painted and I watched.

"In the village?"

"No, the house."

"Since my days as a soldier. This garden has trees I planted myself, and not the youngest ones either. I've known two owners of the villa. Senyora Pepa, a lady with the devil's own temperament and as old as the hills, and her husband Senyor Rovira, a kind-hearted man who never caused anyone any trouble. But the present owners give me free reign to improve the garden, mostly with seasonal flowers; from the very first day they told me to spare no expense."

"You like what I paint?"

"What can I say? No matter how it's done, I still prefer the real thing to any painting of the sea."

And one day he told me to sit down, he was mixing colors and needed my opinion because the light was blinding and it was all flashes and shadows to him, and I almost burned to a crisp out there because he went on and on with his brushstrokes. He was very pleased when I said his color was the color of water without being quite as ethereal. And when I said I had work to do he asked me to stay a while longer. I wanted to be polite, so I did.

Miranda played up to him and tried to woo him. She said he should paint her in front of the rhododendrons. He had already told me he would paint me without my having to ask. Miranda would stand in front of him making faces and striking poses, asking him what he preferred, until one day he said he didn't have time to paint her, but he would do a line drawing. He made her stand there for more than an hour, and he kept reprimanding her, telling her she wasn't still. The girl looked like she had turned to wood, she hardly dared to breathe. When he showed her the finished drawing, she ran off in a rage. Feliu had drawn a toad.

Senyoreta Maragda said that if she were mistress of the house she would fire Miranda on the spot. She was pretty and she was dangerous, and however much she tried, Maragda just didn't like the girl. It seems Senyoreta Rosamaria had replied that she was fond of danger. She wasn't going to do anything about it and she was not afraid. Senyoret Francesc, when his wife was present, had eyes for nothing else. "Yes, it's true," Feliu said one day. "You can see how taken he is with her, more than I imagined at first, when that thing with Eugeni happened."

Some French friends of theirs also came that year, with their daughter. They stayed at the inn run by Bergadans, but they were here all day long. The girl would water-ski, and her mother would go into the kitchen sometimes and prepare a special dish. I enjoyed all their comings and goings, but it messed up my garden, so I had to ask Senyoreta to tell them, in the nicest of ways, that if they wanted flowers I would pick them myself, because the way they were plucking them, they were ruining the plants. The young girl fell in love with Feliu. Although maybe I shouldn't call it love . . . what I mean is she followed him like a shadow. Everywhere he went, she went. She said she wanted to learn to paint, and the French gentleman asked Feliu if he would give his daughter lessons over the summer, and Feliu was forced to agree so he wouldn't offend Senyoret Francesc and his wife, but really he couldn't stand the girl, or her father, or the whole heavenly court of them. So there was the girl, dragging around her easel and her box of paints. And the best part was that her father kept meddling and offering advice to poor Feliu, who was fuming. He said to me: "The first thing would be for this angelic creature to learn how to draw." But what they wanted, the girl and her parents, was to see lots of colors. The day I told Quima about this she hardly listened to me; that was the day she pointed out that Senyoreta only mingled with her own friends. In the morning they swam, and then they set off for the nearby villages and stayed there for lunch. The gentlemen went their own way, so to speak, and the ladies did the same. And Miranda went back to her business . . . this time with Senyoret Francesc.

Toward the end of the summer, Senyoret came to tell me they would be giving a big party before leaving and he asked me to remove the flowerbeds between the two magnolias. I thought I hadn't understood him. "Sorry, what was that?" I asked. He said it again, and I had trouble overcoming my surprise.

"Now that the Peruvian lilies and Dutch pansies are blooming? . . . or do you suppose a flowerbed in full bloom is like a chair, and you can just move it around as you please?"

I had no choice but to dig it up, and where the flowerbeds had been they set up a table that went from one tree to the other, a good ten meters long.

The following day I was keeping myself busy with the Indian carnations and enjoying the scent they gave off, that pleasant bitterness, when Quima approached me wiping her hands on her apron. The first piece of news she spat out was: "Seems they're going to hire extra help."

"What kind?"

"We'll have to see." And with that she turned around and left in a sulk. Senyoreta told her that on the day of the party she would only have to wash and dry the dishes. And do her utmost to see they didn't run out of ice.

The land around the new villa was an abandoned field then, with tall grasses and lizards and those little musical things: crickets, I mean. Well, on the day of the party it was covered in automobiles. The ski instructor dressed up as a thief, a bunch of skeleton keys dangling from his belt. They all wore costumes. The French girl was a butterfly, yellow and blue, and her mother was a deviless. The electricians had been by two days earlier to string up lights in the garden, and the week before, Senyoreta Maragda, the seamstress, had a group of girls from her shop come to the house and they all holed up on the second floor making dresses for the party. And there was a lot of dashing down to Barcelona to buy lace and ribbons; something or other was always missing, and Quima and Mariona were in a frenzy with all the work that had suddenly landed in their laps. Three days before the party the downpours started. Just as soon as one thing was ready . . . down came the rain. The sea, something furious; Feliu with the parasitical little girl trailing him everywhere; the masters in a foul mood; the ski instructor at Can Bergadans with the French gentleman, playing cards all day; the girls sewing away; and everyone glancing uneasily at the sky. The Jerusalem artichokes behind my house were leveled, the motorboat came untied and they had to row out to retrieve it, and it just about cost the fellow with the skis his life because the sea was churning like crazy. I shut myself indoors; from time to time

I would gaze out the window, and when the rain let up I ventured outdoors to have a look around and see what calamities had befallen my garden. At night, glug, glug, glug down the drainpipes.

The last night of rain was fierce. Thunder and lightning like they were being given away. I couldn't sleep. I kept my window open and I could see the trees and the eucalyptus swaying back and forth. The weakest leaves fell to the ground, and my ceiling began to leak in a couple of places. In the early hours everything grew calm and the rain fell steady and gentle. At ten o'clock the sun came out like a prince and the sea turned blue.

The party began with fireworks. Senyoreta Rosamaria came to request that I kindly open the car doors for guests and ask them to leave their vehicles in the field by the house so they wouldn't be in the way. She said the fireworks crew had permission to set up their things in my house. They filled the dining room with crates of rockets, and if a fire had broken out the whole place would have been blown to smithereens.

Everybody knows what fireworks are of course, but it seemed to me that in all the world there couldn't have been a display quite like that evening's. It lasted half an hour, watch in hand. Daisies and stars and many-colored bouquets. One of the shapes was a constellation of stars, and for a minute they lingered high in the sky without dissolving, and I almost passed out because, without realizing it, I had been holding my breath. Feliu came to join me.

"Enjoying yourself?"

"What a party!"

"You do know the reason behind this whole evening . . ."

I had to admit I did not, and he told me that Senyoreta Rosamaria was expecting and Senyoret Francesc wanted to mark the occasion.

"Who would've thought."

There was a sudden chain of blasts, and rockets going off, and we both crouched at the same time; flecks of fire rained down on us. Just at that moment Senyoret Francesc showed up. He looked angry.

"What are you doing here?"

"Ah. Nothing much, just having a look."

"I asked you to be up by the entrance. Remember? More guests have arrived and they've just parked their car in the middle of the garden."

Feliu and I went to take a look at the car, and he climbed in and drove it to the open field. On the way back we walked through the crowd. The musicians were already playing and everyone was dancing, and I spotted the extra help standing beneath the magnolia trees, behind the table. They were driving poor Quima berserk. There were six of them, all dressed in black with shiny lapels, their hair thick with pomade. And suddenly I remembered I was supposed to be at the entrance and I raced over fast as lightning, and I stood there until eleven o'clock. That seemed long enough to me. Then I went back to watch the dancing and had a closer look at the hired waiters. They had been brought up from Barcelona and were very good at serving the guests what they requested, and with impeccable manners. Senyoreta Rosamaria was disguised as a princess, with smoke-colored veils encrusted with sparkling gems, her hair loose. Finally I tired of all the commotion and went down to the belvedere, but Senyoret was there in a skeleton costume, along with two gentlemen in silk capes, and from what I could tell they were talking about the storm and the motorboat they had been forced to tow back while everything around them raged. I headed to my little house; from the window in the back came the sound of someone's conversation. The espadrilles I had on didn't make any noise, so I crept right up to them. It was Senyoreta Eulàlia and Maragda.

"I don't know what more he could want. Would you have married him?"

"What kind of question is that? I hope something comes of this."

"Such as?"

I couldn't repress a cough. They stopped talking and left.

I was almost asleep when Quima came rushing in to find me. Would I kindly lend a hand in the kitchen; with all the dishes that needed washing, they could hardly keep up. She hadn't been allowed to roast the chickens herself, and she was mortally offended. The spread on the table under the magnolias was a real feast. Mountains of chicken. Piles of dry sausage and ham, cooked and serrano. And bologna and all kinds of delicacies, and peeled prawns dipped in mayonnaise. The guests would say, I'll have this, but not that. If they felt like helping themselves, they did, and if they couldn't be bothered, the hired men served them. And the champagne flowed freely. The little French girl drank too much, and apparently around midnight she was carried off to bed, quite dizzy and with her butterfly wings crushed. A lady started to sing and dance, and everyone gathered around and applauded because she was very good. At one in the morning a group of them went down to the beach for a swim and a laugh. I helped out in the kitchen as best I could, which wasn't much. A couple of hours drying dishes and then I said I'd had enough and was going to bed because I had my work cut out for me the following day, trying to fix the mess the guests had made of my garden. And when I was on the point of falling asleep for the second time I heard a sweet voice calling: "Open up, open the door. Are you asleep?"

I pulled on my trousers as fast as I could and found myself face to face with Senyoreta, who had brought me a plate piled high with food.

"It's the least we can do. You should have been included tonight! And very wrong of Quima to make you dry the dishes."

She left, and a moment later I heard footsteps along the dirt path and then bang, bang on the door. A man's voice asking: "Are you the gardener?"

"I am," I said, my mouth full.

"I'm leaving you a bottle by the door, you hear?"

I went out to get the bottle; it was champagne, uncorked. One of the hired men had brought it to me. And suddenly I heard a thud. I raced over and the man was on the ground. I helped him up but he was limping. Being from Barcelona, apparently he didn't know how to walk in the dark.

I ate everything on my plate, though I was more sleepy than hungry. I finished it sitting on the doorstep, by the light of the moon that was scaling the eucalyptus. It had appeared from behind the belvedere railing, a red moon that seemed to herald more rain.

"Is that your dinner?" It was Feliu again, who was also having something to eat.

I showed him the bottle.

"Look what they brought me."

Then the French girl appeared from out of nowhere and Feliu

stood up and fled through the Jerusalem artichokes. The girl stopped in front of me.

"*Bona nit*," she greeted me.

Apparently she had learned a few words in Catalan. She sat down beside me, quiet as a fish. A while later her father came along—he must have been looking for her everywhere—and he dragged her away. He was dressed as a chef, and seeing as how he was on the hefty side, the costume suited him. As soon as he disappeared: Feliu again.

"You're not going to like this," he said.

"What?"

"They've trampled your coronillas."

We hurried to take a look. They say misfortunes never come singly. The coronillas, crushed. The many-leaved lupines as well. It would all have to be thrown out, as if a plant were some kind of tool, and if it breaks you just buy another and replace it. People were still dancing, and there I was with all that blood that had rushed to my head. A few of the guests had gone inside, and through the open window we could see Senyoret Francesc playing billiards with the ski instructor. Three gentlemen were standing around watching them. Senyoret, in his skeleton costume, cut a rather sinister figure behind the green lampshade. Miranda entered with a tray of glasses and bottles of liqueur. As soon as she put the tray down, one of the men who was standing approached her and lifted her apron; she swatted his fingers away and the gentleman left her alone. Miranda gathered up the empty glasses, but she couldn't collect them all because they wouldn't fit on her tray. I tripped on something soft. It was an arm that belonged to one of the guests, who had fallen asleep in the grass. The man groaned.

It was a crazy night. But it all ended well. The sun was rising when I fell asleep, and the house seemed dead. They spent the day in bed.

The following morning, while I was pulling up the lupines and seeing if I could save the coronillas, a van stopped at the gate and a man seated beside the driver got out and rang the bell. He left a lot of parcels and said it was all paid for. The packages were filled with flippers and goggles to wear underwater. There were some snorkels too.

Feliu and I went down to the belvedere for a while. The water was limpid and we could follow all the swimmers' movements. Senyoreta Rosamaria had gone in, too. Four days later they had made a lot of progress and they ventured farther away to sunbathe. When they had mastered the technique to their satisfaction they left for Barcelona. And goodbye until the following year.

They must have been gone a month or so. One afternoon I was standing near the entrance examining some plants that weren't faring too well, distracted enough that I didn't hear him approach.

"Do you happen to know if it's for sale?"

It was a gentleman past middle-age, smartly dressed, with a flushed complexion and thick white hair.

"Excuse me?" I said, turning around.

"I'd like to know if this land is for sale." The man was speaking to me from behind where the boxwood hedge is now.

"I couldn't say," I replied as I pushed back my cap. I knew the land used to belong to old Senyor Farreres, who had lived in Tarragona for many years and died a wealthy man. He was survived by a son. But this son had never been seen in the village. "It's been this way for as long as I can remember, this field, as if the land didn't belong to anyone."

"Is there anyone I might speak to about buying it?"

After mulling it over for a good while, I gave him the name of the old man who had died; perhaps his son was still living, I said, and that was all the information I could provide. The man pulled out a little notebook and wrote down what I told him, and then he asked me the name of the family I worked for. I gave him the name, though I didn't really want to, and still he wouldn't leave. He asked if it was a peaceful village, if the people there were good people, and so on and so forth. After he had made me divulge all that information, he told me he had left for South America as a young man, seeking his fortune, and he had made lots of money. He had a daughter who was very spoiled, she was to be married at the end of the year, and in order to please her he was looking for property in this village, one with a garden by the sea.

II

THE SECOND SUMMER THEY ALL ARRIVED AT THE SAME TIME. The first thing I learned was that Senyoreta Rosamaria had lost the child on Three Kings' Day, the Feast of the Epiphany, and even though several months had passed she was still very pale. The ladies of the house spent their afternoons conversing together. Feliu continued to paint, but his seas were wilder now, as if he had grown angrier at the canvas, and the globs of paint were such that it looked like he was piling on cement. Senyoret Francesc dragged himself around the garden, but mostly he stayed indoors. We could say that year was Miranda's year.

Soon they grew bored, and to distract themselves they had the ski instructor come up. He arrived by land as they had, and he too seemed spiritless. They bought a red boat, a rowboat, because they said rowing was good exercise. And just as soon as they had said this they began their excursions by car, and after that they were never home.

One morning, as I was planting a bed of angel trumpets and pulmonarias, a couple of trucks arrived with a master builder, masons, and a few pick and shovel laborers, and they started laying the foundation for the new villa next door. And when the foundation was moving along, the gentleman who had made his fortune in the Americas, a man by the name of Bellom, returned. He was wearing a white linen suit with a pink carnation in his lapel. The pulmonarias were looking somewhat stunted, and I replaced them with veronicas, not without worrying that their shadow might ruin my angel trumpets. Senyor Bellom went around pestering everyone, as if he were going to build the villa himself. That first day he said to me: "What are you planting?" Veronicas, I said.

He came morning and afternoon, and we always talked. One day he told me his wife had died in childbirth. Then he removed a crumpled piece of paper from his pocket and immediately put it back. "I've just had a letter," he said. "She's only twenty years old and she's the spitting image of her mother. Same eyes, same hair. As for her character, she takes after me. Next week she will have been married six months."

"I've never had children," I said. "I'm rather glad of that. There's already enough misery in this world."

At first the villagers were intimidated by Senyor Bellom. Then they came to respect him, they said he was a good man. In the end they paid him no attention at all. When he was done talking about his daughter he began to tell me about his wife, saying that the world had never seen a man as in love as he had been. What he had experienced, no one else had. It's true that when he spoke of his wife his eyes misted over.

One afternoon I walked him to the eucalyptus and I explained that it had been in the garden since before most of the houses in the village were built. "This tree," I said, "has witnessed much grief and much joy. And it does not change. It has taught me to be what I am, with each leaf like a sickle, and each bud a lead box holding a velvety red flower." The garden was darker then, more remote than it is today. Senyor Bellom's villa, so new and so white, with the shutters painted black and red, and the garden denuded of trees, had spoiled things, though it's difficult to say exactly what had been spoiled.

The day of the eucalyptus I took Senyor Bellom to my little house with the craggy rocks behind it and the pine trees on top. I told him I had lived there since my time as a soldier. An entire life serving the family . . . The rooftop terrace had no railing, no stairs to reach it, so I built a wooden staircase and spent the warmest nights up there, enveloped by the scent of honeysuckle and listening to the nightingale that nested nearby. And almost without realizing it I began to tell Senyor Bellom my story.

"I came into the world by the grace of the Holy Spirit," I said. "That's what my mother told everyone."

Senyor Bellom gave a little laugh and said: "Go on."

"And my mother used to say: 'My son cannot imagine how dearly I paid to have him: it cost me a fissure two fingers long. And we still don't know how it happened in the first place, because as soon as I was in pain I would start weeping and my husband would become discouraged and that was it.' And my father said to me: 'Son, you are a miracle child. It seems you were determined to come into this world no matter what.'"

I was born at noon with a cross on the roof of my mouth. The whole village came to look at it. As a child I spent my days with my mouth agape. My mother always kept me clean and tidy, ready to be put on display. Open your mouth, so they can see the cross. Senyor Bellom listened quietly as I told him my story, and if I stopped he would say: "Go on, go on." And I continued. When I grew old enough to think, I was always fearful inside because I was so different from everyone else. If I went out to play in front of the house, the children on the street would surround me and ask me to show them the cross. One morning, when I was a little older, I found myself home alone with a cold. I went to the mirror, threw back my head, and opened my mouth. And I didn't see anything. It's true that no one had mentioned the cross for some time. I thought that maybe grown-ups' eyes see things differently than children's eyes. And later I thought something else: that the cross had slowly faded as I lost my innocence.

But what Senyor Bellom most liked was hearing me talk about Cecília. That first day at my house he paused in front of the rocking chair. "Cecília's rocking chair," I said. "And that ribbon on the banister was the ribbon she used to tie up her hair." Senyor Bellom said: "Cecília was your wife?" "Yes, and she had such a mass of hair, and it was so fine, that if she didn't tie it up it was unmanageable, and hairpins couldn't hold it." I showed him the shelf with my little kerosene lamp. "I light it every Friday." Behind the oil lamp, the photograph of Cecília, and in front of it a pebble. Senyor Bellom picked up the photograph, looked at it for a while, and put it back. "But what is a picture without the love that was reflected in her gaze, her voice, her manner of speaking?" I said.

I didn't tell him, because I was afraid of being tiresome, that Cecília always wore lavender dresses. Little lavender gingham dresses. But from a distance the dresses looked like they were a solid color: lavender. She had small greenish eyes, deep-set and bright. She was more short than tall, very thin, with a flat stomach. She had olive skin, darker in summer. Her loveliest feature was her hair: sun golden, waterfall long. When I came back from the cemetery I pounded the eucalyptus tree until I bled. "Would you like to comb my hair?" she would ask me. And she would sit down and I would comb her hair with a honey-colored comb. And when we had pretend fights in bed, sometimes I would tie her hair around my neck and we would laugh. We were one. Like the eucalyptus, I had lived my life tall and calm. My arms strong in their sockets, my feet firm on the ground. And at the moment of her death . . . she died in my arms, in my hands you might say, like a little bird . . . the whole of me shattered. As if someone had smashed me to bits and strewn the pieces about.

Two years elapsed before I told her she should be mine. She worked in the house, back in Senyora Pepa's days; she had been hired to help the housemaid. The first time I laid eyes on her in her lavender dress, her hair so blond . . . maybe no one would believe me, but I loved her for two years and she never knew. When we crossed paths I didn't look at her. But I felt her.

Arranging flowers in vases is what brought us together. Senyora Pepa had given her that chore. I would deliver the flowers to the house, leaving them on the table on the veranda, and she would put together the bouquets and go around decorating every room with all the splendor I brought in from the garden. One day, as I was setting down the basket of flowers on the table, someone rang the doorbell and she ran to answer it. But first she removed her apron. And I picked it up and did something bad. I looked to see what she had in the pockets. I found a pebble and I kept it. It was the first thing I had of hers. I would put it in my mouth while I worked, like you would a piece of candy. It might be hard to understand how taken I was with her . . . but you see, she was sixteen when I met her, and I was almost thirty-five.

One morning, as I was making a little bouquet of grape hyacinths, she asked me why I was laughing. "I don't know," I said. "When I see you I'm filled with joy." That's how it was, as soon as I saw her a kind of sweetness enveloped me.

But I haven't explained how the story of the pebble started. The afternoon was grey with clouds, and I was pruning the rosebushes. I spotted her from a distance. She was on her way back from sweeping the belvedere and she was strolling along slowly. Then a downpour broke out and she sheltered beneath a mulberry tree. I left my work and sought cover beside her. We were talking about the rain and suddenly she grew silent, as if enchanted by something. She was looking at a pebble by her feet. She picked it up and put it in her pocket without a word. It was white, it *is* white, but it seemed whiter then because it was wet from the rain, and the black strip around it seemed darker too. Once dry it's not so very white, nor the line so very black. The rain stopped and she ran off.

She died nearly twenty years ago. More than a few other women have been sweet on me! Many more. Here at the house and elsewhere, in the village. But it was no good: they were simply women. It defies explanation. She wasn't a woman. She was tenderness itself.

But I should tell you more about the masters.

In fair weather they breakfasted outside, beneath the magnolia trees. When the weather was bad, they took their breakfast on the veranda. The windows there were hung with blue silk curtains, and in the summer, when a breeze made them shiver ever so gently, they looked like flags. They referred to the veranda as the steamship, and all the windowsills were ringed with blue hydrangeas on the inside, the fountain in the center too, but it was almost never turned on. Senyora Pepa preferred to have late tulips there, the ones with the ruffle.

It was on account of a flowerpot that Senyoret and I had a bit of a run-in. One night I was sitting at the entrance to my house when I heard what sounded like a stifled laugh. I thought I glimpsed two shadows on the linden promenade. My curiosity was piqued and I went to have a turn higher up and entered the promenade by the upper path, but they were already near the belvedere. When I arrived, they had gone down to the beach. I leaned over the railing and concealed myself behind a flowerpot. They had headed left, to where the beach ends by the rocks. It was a peaceful night, not too dark, and the sky was dotted with flickering stars. Slowly, from the mass of shadows I was able to make out the two figures. Senyoret and Miranda lying together! I was so absorbed spying on them that I accidently elbowed the flowerpot and it went over the railing. I couldn't get away fast enough.

The following day, as I was preparing my lunch, I heard someone enter the dining room. I came out from the kitchen, and there was Senyoret in his striped robe.

"*Bon dia.*"

He stood there for a moment without opening his mouth. After he had looked at me long and hard he said: "A flowerpot in the belvedere fell down to the beach. You'll need to clean up the pieces before someone gets hurt."

"A flowerpot?" I said, all innocent, but I saw immediately that he wasn't amused.

"It fell last night. And there was no wind."

And then something happened: without intending to, we both looked at each other and sized the other up, and we struggled not to laugh. What I mean is that something flashed across our eyes and the corners of our mouths trembled a little.

"It fell straight down from the railing." He started acting distracted and pretended to look at the ceiling, and he said: "Nice weather, last night."

To avoid having to answer, I asked him if he had decided what to do with the flowerpots. He had to think about it.

"What flowerpots?"

"The ones with the camellias. You said you wanted camellias below the veranda, planted in the ground, and I told you we would have to buy chestnut soil. Remember?"

"Ah yes, as you wish. My wife agrees we should move the camellias." He blushed when he uttered the words *my wife*. "But she says that if they won't fare well in the ground she would prefer to keep them in the flowerpots, even if the effect isn't as nice."

He turned toward the door, but he seemed undecided. And when I least expected it he wheeled around and from his pocket he pulled a crumpled piece of paper, which I immediately recognized as money. He slipped the bill under the salad dish and left, saying: "Very well, then."

I was offended. But when it occurred to me to run after him and return the money, it was too late. I knew they all went down to the beach early in the morning, but he never did before noon. The following day I walked to the house around that same time, feeling certain I would find him reading the newspaper. I entered. The fountain on, the water flowing gently. He and Miranda in an embrace.

The first thing I saw was Miranda's head between Senyoret's shoulder and his hair. He had his back to me. I don't know how long I stood there. I couldn't say if it was a long time or only a moment. Enough for me to back away. I never knew if Miranda told him she had seen me. But the vision of Miranda's head stayed on my retina all day; it was like a severed head.

The next day I went back, with better luck. He was in his chair, reading. As soon as I entered he glanced at me and asked if the manure had been delivered yet. He meant the chestnut soil of course. I said it had not, and straight away, so he couldn't make some other senseless comment, I handed him the banknote.

"You dropped this the other day."

He played dumb.

"What was that?"

"This money is yours."

I gave it to him. He looked at it as if he didn't understand, and he said I was mistaken.

"It's yours. You forgot it the day you came to tell me that the flowerpot had fallen down. You left it on the table."

He was silent for a moment; you could tell his mind was churning.

"It was for the extra work of gathering up all the bits of broken flowerpot."

He said it so fast and with such fury that I turned and walked away without even opening my mouth.

That night, I was sitting outside my door when Quima came around.

"You'll never guess."

"What? Where?"

"Right here in this family. It seems once she knew for certain that she was expecting, Senyoreta refused. That's why she looks like a ghost. There was a terrible rift, because he wanted a child. And they were so smitten just last year! So he took off alone and roamed the world for two months. As if they had separated."

"And how did you find out?"

"The mulatto girl."

"Don't believe it then."

When I thought she was done she came over and whispered in my ear:

"Senyoreta wanted to get rid of her but Senyoret wouldn't hear of it; he said she was a nice girl. And Senyoreta, so she wouldn't have to come out and say why she had never warmed to Miranda, let it go. How does this one end?"

"How do you think? Trust me and forget about it."

"You sure he's not serious about her?"

Before leaving she said she had heard that Senyoreta Eulàlia's husband was coming up.

"I didn't know she was married."

"No? And guess what he does? He hunts lions. Things rich people do."

Senyoreta told her all about it one day. It seems they were madly in love when they married, but, the usual, over the years they tired of each other. But they had loved each other once so they didn't want to separate, and to amuse themselves they went to Africa, to hunt lions. Senyoreta Eulàlia stayed there a couple of years to keep her husband company, up and down the mountains and crossing over rivers, but finally she had enough and returned. And they were quite happy that way. They would see each other from time to time, and it seems there was love between them. He would come to Barcelona and she would go to Africa. And with all their comings and goings they managed to make it work.

I had never seen anyone like Senyoret Sebastià. He must have been about thirty-five, a well-preserved thirty-five. Sometimes when he laughed, he roared, and then he looked about twenty. Blond hair, slate eyes. Very thin, very tall. Deep wrinkles around his mouth, from being sad and lonely in Africa, Quima said, but I'm sure it was from all that laughing. He brought back a small lion, and two zebroid skins that he immediately hung on the walls. And a lot of merriment. A lot of hustle and bustle. They commissioned the blacksmith to make a cage for the lion, with a little sleeping shelter. It was a first-rate animal, beautiful and calm, that devoured huge hunks of meat. It had lustrous fur and glassy, sun-dappled eyes. It looked rather bored and slept like a log. Some evenings I would keep him company for a while. I would sit by the cage and he would come to see me, stare at me; some days he would sit close to where I was, other days he would lie on the far side of the cage. Sometimes he was very playful.

So there we were: with a lion in a cage, skins on the walls, and a long stretch of summer before us. Senyoret Sebastià might have been a hunter, but he swam like a fish. We immediately struck up a friendship, and the first time we had a real conversation he said he would bring me back seeds and plants from that country that would make my jaw drop. One in particular, the name eluded him, was a kind of sunflower the color of fire that closed up if you looked at it too long.

Sebastià hadn't been at the house fifteen days when he came looking for me one night and told me to follow him if I wanted a good laugh. We rounded the back of the house and stopped beneath the ski instructor's balcony; from the railing hung a very long rope, and I still remember the scent of the pittosporums in bloom, so pungent it could knock you over. "Help me pull on that rope," he said in a low voice. The two of us got busy. At first it was hard going, but then the rope came fast, and suddenly it caught on something. "Give it all you've got!" The shouting began upstairs. "Now run!" And we ran to my house, and once we were inside I asked him what had happened. And it seems he had crept into the ski instructor's bedroom while the fellow was sleeping and he had tied the rope around the bed frame. "On the quiet, the way the blacks hunt rhinoceros." And the shouting had been the instructor, who had suddenly found himself on the balcony, bed and all. He had been jolted awake when the bedstead bumped into the threshold.

Senyoret Sebastià was the oldest, the others were just kids really, but he was the most fun. Some days he went around like he had gone half mad. On another occasion he came for me at two in the morning. "Here, take the camera," he said, handing me a photographic camera. He was barefoot and in shorts. We made our way to the house in the dark, and when we were inside he turned on a flashlight and we climbed the stairs. We stopped on the landing in front of Senyoreta Maragda's door. "Hold the magnesium lamp and hand me the camera." He said the magnesium would frighten them even more. We opened the door: the balcony wide open, a touch of starlight streaming in. Senyoret Sebastià turned on the little flashlight to get his bearings and he photographed Senyoreta Maragda, who let out a bloodcurdling scream and sat up in bed. After taking her picture he tried to placate her with kind words, for she was livid, and he got her to come with us. The three of us headed to Feliu's room. He was snoring. Sebastià started to pester him with the flashlight and Feliu, who was lying on his side, waved his hand as if brushing away a fly. Then he turned on his back. We took his picture while he was asleep. When we were almost to the door we heard him mutter in a low voice: "You animals." We made the rounds and photographed everyone. Senyoreta Eulàlia was angrier than the rest, because she was awake reading, naked from head to toe. She was so furious with her husband that she hurled a bottle of water at his head and chased after us in the worst possible way.

It was great fun.

One day when Miranda was serving breakfast, Senyoret Sebastià asked her if she liked the beach, and she said she preferred swimming in the river: salt water got up her nostrils and it was unpleasant. They all began to ask her to go down to the beach with them, and Senyoret Sebastià said he would hold her up so she wouldn't get water in her nose. Senyoreta Maragda took Miranda with her and lent her one of her bathing costumes. I didn't hear about this right away. Sometimes I found out about things a few days later, but there was always someone who filled me in. Apparently Senyoret was beside himself that morning trying to find Miranda, asking Quima and Mariona where she had got to. By the time he set foot on the beach it was already half past twelve. It seems that when he saw Miranda there with the group of them, he went chalk white. But he hid his feelings as best he could and he even managed a witty remark.

That afternoon Feliu found me transferring the camellias from the flowerpots.

"I can't say I like the way they carry on. I've never been keen on Miranda but I've tried to keep the peace. All of this puts me off."

He asked me what I was doing with all that dark soil, and I told him. He helped me remove the camellias from the flowerpots. He was sulking. But he let himself be drawn in, and a few days later he was the first to play up to Miranda. They had her with them all day long, and they hired a young girl from the village to do her work. "In the end she'll leave," Quima said. "She'll be made to." I didn't see it that way, but some people live on hope. And Miranda allowed Senyoret Sebastià to court her. It's what everyone wanted. A distraction. And one day Senyoreta Eulàlia said: "Perhaps my husband is doing too good a job of this play-acting." But it seems she was easily appeased, and in the end she said she preferred that little twinge in her heart to having him away, down there, always fearing he might be eaten by a tiger.

The entire village was abuzz with the Miranda affair, and the family was excoriated for weaving a housemaid into their summer life. It's the kind of thing that pleases no one. Everyone has their place. I said to Quima: "It will run its course; this is just a bad summer, better not make too much of it." But the thing is, after two or three weeks with Miranda up on a pedestal, they said Senyoret Francesc had gone into Barcelona on some business with his financial advisor. My first thought was he had left so he wouldn't end up throttling all of them. And their little mischief let up some, but it didn't stop altogether, and Miranda still allowed herself to be fussed over. But without Senyoret things were more subdued of course, and they were not in such a frenzy.

And then one day Quima came to see me.

"Have you heard? Senyoret Francesc has been in the village for two days now. He's driving around in a plum-colored automobile that's ten meters long. And you know where he's living? He's taken a room at Can Bergadans."

"I'm not surprised," I said, just so she would leave me alone.

That same day Feliu, Senyoret Sebastià, and Senyoreta Eulàlia came looking for me. It was plain they didn't know where to begin. Senyoreta Eulàlia walked over to Cecília's shelf and said: "Lovely, this little pebble." I didn't reply and she understood at once that I didn't like her nosing about in my things.

"Well . . ." Feliu began.

"You probably know that my husband . . ."

"We wanted to ask you . . . since you're like family to us . . . Francesc got all worked up a few days ago, for no reason at all, and he stormed off to Barcelona, and now he's gone to live at Can Bergadans. . . He likes to play jokes, but he can't stand for them to be played on him."

"Last night we went looking for him, with Feliu and Eulàlia," said Senyoret Sebastià. He hadn't opened his mouth until then. "We were courteous with him but he kicked us out quite unceremoniously. Will you go? Maybe he'll listen to you. He holds you in high esteem."

I immediately understood they were trying to pull one on me. On me and on Senyoret. They must have really laughed imagining the look on Senyoret's face when he saw me. I was disappointed they thought me so naïve, and I was on the verge of telling them to leave me in peace. But the truth is down deep I was amused.

"Well, if you think I should . . ."

Before going upstairs, Senyor Bergadans had me drink a glass of anisette. And as he was putting the top back on the bottle he winked at me.

"You're here for the gentleman upstairs, no? Are you sure they're not going to put them all away one of these days?"

"They're young."

I went up. Sweat oiled my neck and my hands were sticky on the banister. When I got upstairs I knocked on the door and waited a while. I knocked again, and again. Not a sound. Then it occurred to me that Senyoret might have gone out, unseen by Bergadans, and I went back downstairs.

"No answer. You think he's upstairs but who knows where he might be."

He scratched the back of his neck, a habit of his, and then he started laughing for no reason.

"He's up there. I would've seen him walk by. I haven't budged from behind the counter."

I could barely make out what he was saying, he was laughing

so hard. When I thought he was about to choke he said: "Knock harder, he might be asleep."

I went back up. I knocked on the door, quite hard, and finally I turned the knob; the door was unlocked, and there I stood. Through the window you could see the calm sea, and to the left, the canopy of linden and mulberry trees in our garden. Farther out there was the red rowboat with someone in it, and I thought I recognized Senyoreta Eulàlia.

Senyoret Francesc was stretched out on the bed, sort of crosswise, and his feet stuck out over the mattress. He was asleep with his mouth open. I entered, shut the door behind me, and I went over to him and gave him a little shake. The sound of the rain might have had a similar effect. So I left and slammed the door. Bergadans, from downstairs, cried out: "Hey, watch it!"

I went back in and he had rolled over. His forehead was beaded with sweat. I didn't know what to do, so I sat in a chair in the corner and observed the objects around me: the crocheted bedspread, the washbasin with the iron stand, the desk with an empty inkwell and a pink blotter. On the nightstand there was a glass and a bottle with a drawing of a horse on the label. And as I was studying the horse, he woke up.

He hardly recognized me at first.

"What are you doing here?" he said, propping himself up, one elbow on the pillow.

"You can see for yourself . . ."

"Is there something you need?"

He bolted upright and wiped his lips with the back of his hand. Then he poured himself some juice and gulped it down.

"No Senyor, no."

"So you're here to sit vigil then? If it's company you think I need . . ." He placed both feet on the floor and gave me a nasty look. "They must have sent you. I wouldn't put it past them. Who told you I was here?"

"You think the whole village doesn't know?"

"They must have a lot of time on their hands."

Then he flew into a sudden rage, grabbed the bottle, and smashed it against the wall. When he saw the large splatter it left he grumbled, and you could tell he didn't know what to say. He pointed his finger at me.

"You must find me very childish." He fished a cigarette from his pocket and seemed to calm down. "You think I'm in any mood for a visit? What are you doing in that chair?"

"I meant no disrespect. I sat down without thinking." I stood up.

"No, no, you can sit. Have you been here long?"

"No, not long. But I couldn't seem to wake you."

"They made you come, didn't they? They must be in need of a laugh."

"It's no good to live away from one's home."

"Ah no? Well, then!"

I felt things had dragged on too long and I slowly walked to the door.

"What should I tell them?"

"That you couldn't find me." He tossed the cigarette out the window and turned to face me. "Tell them you couldn't find me," he repeated.

Of course they didn't believe me. A few days later I spotted

Senyoret Francesc strolling beneath the mulberry trees with Feliu, as if nothing had happened. That afternoon Quima told me that as soon as lunch was over they had all hurried off. They were on their way to France to see a play that was being performed in a castle.

Only the servants and Miranda stayed at the house, and none of us knew for sure if Miranda was one of the servants or not. Mariona and I hadn't had any dealings before, but we became friends during those days, because some evenings she would come to see the lion. I spent many an hour in front of the cage, seated in a low chair. Sometimes he sauntered over to us and stared at us as if he were a person, and if we spoke to the lion, he grew still as death. A beautiful creature, he was. I would wait until evening so I could visit him during the quiet hour. And, naturally, I enjoyed it more when I was alone. One day I pushed a branch through the iron bars, just because, and he pounced. I crept away silently and didn't tell anyone. And after that, every evening when I pushed the branch through he would jump. One night I went to the cage later than usual and he was making the saddest of yowls, and as soon as he saw me he grew silent and lumbered over to my side of the cage, and he rubbed his head against the bars with such intent that I would have petted him if he hadn't been a lion, that's how fond of him I was.

We had grown so close that the day Miranda intruded on us I could have strangled her. I told her to go away. She didn't say anything, she just sat on the ground and ruined my evening. Worse than that, the following day she came back and did the stupidest thing. She reached into the cage and grabbed the lion by the ear. I couldn't believe my eyes. Just as I was about to whack her on the arm, she gave a hard tug and started screaming like she had gone mad. The lion was startled and swiped her hand with his paw. She blenched, looked down at her bloody hand, and fainted full length on the ground.

Senyor Bellom came again to check on the work next door. I hadn't laid eyes on him for a month but he greeted me as if he had been there the entire time. All smiles. With a fresh carnation and a suit that looked brand new.

"They don't seem to be in much of a hurry, but I don't mind. What I want is a job well done."

Every morning, if I happened to be working nearby, we had a nice little chat. One day he came at me with a question I wasn't expecting.

"The dark-skinned girl I see in the village sometimes, she works for your masters doesn't she?"

I said she was the first housemaid.

"Do you happen to know what country she's from?"

"Brazil, that's what I hear."

He was quiet for a moment, as if thinking.

"I have business there, in Brazil. I lived there for a couple of years. Nice place, Brazil, nice country."

He glanced at his watch and turned around. The following day he said he was off to Barcelona, and from Barcelona to Paris, and from Paris he would go on to Holland, and farther away still. Before holding out his hand for me to shake, he gave me a cigar so long that with the help of a pair of scissors I was able to make it into three.

They were all back a week later. That first night, I was sleeping on my rooftop terrace and Senyoret Sebastià came up to see me. He sat down beside me but I didn't move, the entire time I peered up at him from below. The night was hot and humid and the scent of honeysuckle filled the air.

"Tell me about the lion biting Miranda."

I said he had only scratched her, and I recounted the whole episode very patiently. He howled with laughter, and frankly, I thought it was excessive. When he collected himself I asked him how the trip had gone.

He said they had driven at over a hundred kilometers an hour the whole time, and they had all been sick after eating lobster that was slightly off. Apparently Senyoret and Senyoreta had made their peace and were back to sleeping together. They strolled along the streets holding hands. The play was nothing to write home about, and they had trouble following it because the acoustics weren't good, so they left early and went to amuse themselves in a café.

One morning Senyoreta Rosamaria came to watch me thinning out the mock oranges.

"Don't you think they're too old?"

I had to explain they could still bloom plenty, all they needed was a bit of pruning. Then, as she glanced over at the work being done next door, she said: "It's sad they're building a house so nearby . . . it'll ruin our view."

I thought she was making too much of it. It was common knowledge that the new villa would only have one floor, but I didn't feel like arguing so I said she was quite right. I mentioned in passing that Senyor Bellom had come by to see the work, and that he had spread the word in the village that he planned to keep two horses, one for his daughter and one for his son-in-law, and he was going to have them brought over from that special country where they bred the best ones. I don't think she liked the idea at all.

Before she left she gave me a nicely wrapped package tied with yellow string.

"A souvenir from France."

And I found myself with a dozen handkerchiefs.

They stayed longer than usual that year. The leaves had already turned and many of the trees were bare. In the evening they lit a fire in the large drawing room. The sea was gradually leached of color and grew rough in the afternoon. Feliu gave up his painting because the wind carried off his easel. He said he wasn't at all pleased with his work that summer.

One afternoon when I was pulling up the marigolds, which had given all they had to give, I heard voices on the belvedere and I spotted Mariona talking to a young mason by the name of Mingo. As soon as she saw me she called out: "Come, come keep us company."

"She's sad because the summer's over," he said.

"That's how it goes . . ."

I left them alone and went to find Senyoret Sebastià, who was with Senyoreta Eulàlia. To put his mind at ease I told him I would take excellent care of the lion in his absence. But it turned out they were taking him with them and giving him to an animal park. He gave me a pat on the back—they all did the same—and he said:

"If you want, I'll bring you half a dozen of them when I come back. With any luck they'll make a meal out of Miranda!"

"Just as long as you remember to bring me the seeds."

Senyoret Francesc gave me a list of instructions before he left. He said when the winter passed he would send workmen to repair the leaks. And painters would come when the workmen had finished. He wanted the house clean as a whistle the following summer.

That was a terrible winter. The workmen who were supposed to come once the winter was over arrived as soon as the masters left. Repairing the leaks was easy, and they soon finished, but they made a mess. Then the painters showed up. They dragged their feet as much as they could. On happy-weather days they went in search of sunlight during their lunch break, and they discovered a secluded spot near my house. I didn't like the kind of young men they were, very brazen. And we know what painters are like: a couple of brushstrokes and a whole lot of whistling. I was fed up with so much whistling.

After that I devoted a few days to resting, to thinking about my plants and rose grafts and wandering about the garden studying how everything might come together. The quietude was broken by a letter from Senyoret. He said he wanted daisies all along the belvedere. And on either side of the main gate, flowerbeds with white roses of the kind that bloomed three times a year. At the very bottom of the letter, after his signature, he mentioned that new workmen would be arriving, and they would eat and sleep at Can Bergadans. He said they would build a stable. I wasn't at all surprised.

You might have mistaken those workmen for lords. One day they asked me if they could use my kitchen, the food at Can Bergadans wasn't up to snuff and they needed proper nourishment. I didn't want to be rude but I had to say no. And it was pure torture, because the stable they were building was near my house and I couldn't get them out of my hair. I stayed indoors so I wouldn't have to see them. I only went out in the morning, before they arrived, and in the evening after they left. And on rainy days when they didn't show their faces.

They built a first-class stable, with two rooms upstairs for the person who would be looking after the horses.

Quima hadn't come for several Sundays in a row because she was caring for a sick lady, and I had to wash my own clothes. The first Sunday she returned she was taken aback by all the changes. I showed her around the freshly painted house, heavenly it was, all white, with a fine gold molding in some rooms. The floors were still dirty from the painters because Senyoret had instructed me to hold off on sending for someone to clean. When Quima saw the stable, she said: "You know what's going on here? They're envious of the neighbors."

After the workmen left I had to deal with the electricians, then more painters for the bathrooms and the stable. It was a constant parade. The coming and going lasted until mid-May. Then Quima had to scramble to find a couple of girls willing to take on the task of cleaning the place. While they were at it, a letter from Senyoret. He said someone would come to collect the old furniture and deliver new furniture. The interior decorator would arrange it all, and I should leave him to his work.

Things finally calmed down, but the flowers were blooming already, and ahead of me lay the arduous task of tending the seedlings and replanting them. And I was worn out.

In the meantime the neighbor's villa continued to rise. Mariona's mason friend told me that some rooms had black marble floors and others had white marble floors. And out front they were going to build a swimming pool a hundred meters long, heated in winter. Everyone was talking about it. One day when I went for a drink, Bergadans told me that one side of the living room would have two glass walls, floor to ceiling, filled with water and fish.

The horses arrived in early June. One was black with a white spot on its forehead and seemed to understand everything. A small, middle-aged man brought them. He would be staying on to look after them. Straightaway he introduced himself as Toni and said he had won many races in his younger years. He had been quite famous. He shook hands with me and everything, but I left as soon as I could get away because he was too pretentious for my taste. He called himself a riding instructor. The horses already had names when they arrived. The black one was Lucifer. The white one, Fletxa. Arrow.

Everyone arrived in late June, the day after the Feast of Saint John.

A novelty: Senyoreta Eulàlia was now a painter. Her creations were strange. She painted people and all, but always tiny and always far away. She also did flowers. She made them true to life and counted the leaves to be sure she hadn't left any out, but even then they didn't look like real flowers. I couldn't say if they were lovelier or not as nice . . . it was hard to explain. Like the colors she used, which seemed lit from within. As soon as I saw her I asked what Senyoret Sebastià was up to. She said he was in Africa and wouldn't be able to come that summer. I was beginning to fear I wouldn't have my seeds. Aside from Senyoreta Eulàlia, who only thought about painting, everyone else talked about Senyor Bellom's house.

"They must be close to finishing now," Feliu said to me one day as we were watching the workmen.

"Now the real work begins."

Mingo was very happy because he had been able to see Mariona.

No one discussed the work that had been done to our villa. Only the horses, but not much about them either. Until they all took up riding that is. But the arrival of the horses couldn't fully eradicate their anguish at being fairly small fry in comparison to Senyor Bellom. The one most incensed about it, though I couldn't see how it was any of her business, was Senyoreta Maragda.

"All we need now is for Senyor Bellom's horses to be better than ours."

They learned to ride. Early in the morning, before going for a swim, they would trot up and down the linden promenade. Senyoret Francesc was a fast learner and he put on airs, as if he was the first person who ever rode a horse, one hand on his waist and head held high. Sometimes, in the evenings, Toni and I talked about it and laughed. We didn't have much in common, but he was a man who grew on you the more you got to know him. His problem was he never missed a chance to act self-important, especially around people he had never seen before. He said Senyoreta Rosamaria would be the best rider because she knew how to become one with the horse. And he was right, although it took her a while to sit up straight, and she latched onto the horse's neck the minute she was scared. But as soon as she overcame her fear she and Fletxa looked like they were one and the same. He was a proud horse and would paw the ground with one foot and shake his head over nothing. Senyoreta came to enjoy riding so much she would even take him out in the afternoons. She brushed him down every day, and as soon as he saw her he would get excited and paw the ground. The distraction rejuvenated Senyoreta, and she was already quite young. There was a different air about her.

"What do you think of my horse?" she would ask every time she saw me.

I liked the other one better, but I couldn't see the harm in pleasing her.

"Handsome, very handsome," I said.

No one mentioned Miranda, even though she was especially beautiful that year. On Sundays she would slip on a green dress and go out. Dancing, she told me. She would come back late and disheveled. But she didn't stroll in the garden at night or swim by moonlight.

"She's changed a lot," Quima said.

The truth is Senyoreta Rosamaria might have looked like an angel, but she was shrewd, and she put a stop to things without making a fuss. The previous summer Miranda had had big ideas, especially with the arrival of Senyoret Sebastià. When she went into the kitchen to play the grand lady, all she could talk about was him. But Quima learned from Mariona that all of a sudden she wanted to return to her country. She said she was starting to grow tired and homesick. Back to the jungle! Right away she and Toni had words. Apparently she was meddling with the horses. Toni was upset. One evening he had been to Can Bergadans for a drink and when he came back she was in the stable stuffing the horse full of sugar. Senyoreta's horse that is. Toni said that, one, he never wanted to see her in the stable again and, two, if she ever gave the horses sugar again, he would whip her until she was crawling on all fours. And to get out of there fast. She left in a hurry and did what she often did, which was to say nothing when you were expecting her to speak. Around that time a letter from her village arrived.

Mariona waited a long time to come to see me. She seemed more of a woman now, and was better dressed. She said in Barcelona she was sent to Senyoreta Maragda's workshop two afternoons a week to learn how to sew, and she liked it, because if she learned then maybe she could be a seamstress instead of having to serve.

"I've made myself a dress already, following a pattern. I'm told that I'm quite good at it."

I asked her how the winter had gone and she said all right; on Sundays she would go to see the animals, and they had lions there, old and very large, not as handsome as Senyoret Sebastià's. You could tell she didn't care for any of it and missed the village.

"How are things with Mingo?"

"It's hard to tell. He's all right, but he's only a laborer, and if he doesn't make more money I don't want to marry him."

She asked me to show her the stable because she hadn't seen it yet, and I said to go find Toni and tell him I had sent her. But she had heard Miranda's story, from Miranda's mouth, and she didn't want to go without me. Toni gave her a warm welcome. He said she could visit the stable any time she wanted to see the horses, even if he wasn't there. He asked only that she not give them sugar. Carob beans, at most. He took her around his little rooms, with the walls covered with pictures of horses and clippings of newspapers and photographs of him in his jockey silks. And he showed her a picture of his son, who was away at a Catholic boarding school. I said I had known Mariona since she was a girl, and now here she was in love with one of Senyor Bellom's masons. And Toni teased her about it to make her blush.

We learned through Mariona that an aunt of Senyoreta Rosamaria's had gone to live with her that winter. Fortunately it was only for a short while. It seems Senyoret Francesc absolutely abhorred her, and one day he said that if she didn't go home he was going to lock her in a wardrobe and leave her there to die. And she, the aunt, overheard him. According to Mariona, it's not that she was doing anything wrong. She was just a poor woman who was always hot and kept opening the balcony doors because the radiators, she said, were too large and the heat gave her a headache. An annoying habit of hers. But she couldn't be reined in. Mariona spent her days closing the doors to the balconies, and some afternoons the apartment was an icebox. One day there was a commotion because the aunt couldn't find her teeth. She wore false teeth, and every night when she climbed into bed she would soak them in a glass of water. They couldn't very well have misplaced themselves. That afternoon, Senyoreta's aunt started saying that one of the servant girls had taken them as a joke, and Senyoret and Senyoreta had them all line up, and Senyoret said that if the dentures belonging to Senyora Antònia, the aunt, didn't turn up, they all had their marching orders, and the girls were very worried. Rosalia, the cook who went back to her village in the summers, said she was fed up with serving in that household and if they were assembled again she would quit on the spot. Mariona was convinced it was Miranda who had taken the teeth, but the following morning when she was dusting the vases she heard Senyoret and Senyoreta laughing in the next room, and as the door was ajar she listened in, and she overheard Senyoret saying he was thinking of taking the dentures to a museum. And they laughed and laughed, because that's the kind of people they were. In the end the aunt was really put out, or maybe she realized what had happened, and she went back to her house, even though as she got older she liked living alone less and less.

Mariona said it was the right thing to do. She didn't belong in that house.

It would have been a calm summer, the calmest of all, had it not been for the monkey. Trouble and discord galore.

One of Miranda's brothers came to visit, the one who had written to her from their village. And he showed up with a she-monkey. He stayed at Can Bergadans for two weeks, and when he went home he left the monkey with Miranda as a souvenir.

Miranda asked Senyoreta's permission to keep the monkey in her room, and Senyoreta was reckless enough to allow it. Everyone wanted to see it, and Senyoreta Maragda stuck her nose where it didn't belong and said they should keep it tied up on the veranda, it would be a source of entertainment. Her name was Tití. And Tití played her part well. She spent the day on a silk cushion, and pranced about every so often, and amused herself easily: she would act like she was reading the newspaper, or clasp her hands together as if in prayer, or lounge on her back belly-up and pretend to sleep, and spy on everything. Sometimes she would hang onto the back of a chair and swing like a pendulum, grabbing on with one hand, then with the other. On rainy days when everyone had tea on the veranda, she would stride up and down holding a tiny umbrella that Senyoreta Maragda had made for her. She was little, I mean in size, and young. Her eyes were alert and full of mischief; I think in all the world there wasn't a monkey with a greater penchant for mischief. The day they asked me if I wanted to see her, she was perched on the back of a chair, very still. I went over to her, but she didn't move. I petted her out of politeness, and while I was speaking to the Senyorets, she untied my espadrilles. I only noticed when I was walking away and nearly tripped.

Soon they were taking the monkey on their walks. They carried her down to the beach, and when Senyoreta Rosamaria went horseback riding she took the monkey along, and Tití would shriek with joy. But the first time they went riding together the monkey was frightened and she latched onto Senyoreta's arm so tightly that she drew blood. Sometimes Miranda would pick up the monkey and take her into the kitchen to feed her. Quima was livid.

"You'll find that here in this country we're not accustomed to this kind of creature."

And Tití all quiet and still, being shown around everywhere, growing as smart as if she had been to school. And then she started acting crazy. One night when it was especially hot and I was having trouble sleeping, I heard the horses by my house, clip-clop, clip-clop, and a kind of mirthful shriek. I went downstairs and there were the two horses, right at my window. She was leading one by the rope. When she realized I was about to pounce on her she ran for it.

I went to wake Toni.

"This monkey is starting to take too many liberties."

He agreed with me, but he advised me not to tell the masters; it wasn't worth it, and it might give Miranda a reason to laugh.

Eight days later the house flooded. The girls and Quima realized what was happening when water started pouring down the kitchen stairs. They found all the faucets in the bathtubs and sinks turned on; water had been running all morning while the family were down on the beach with the horses.

"I don't understand," Feliu said. "If it were just one faucet . . . and I don't want to be suspicious, but I wonder if behind all this . . . see where I'm going? The monkey might have turned on one of the faucets, but not all of them I don't think."

I had hardly seen him in the last month. He was painting little. That day he was seated in front of his easel. And all of sudden he asked me what I thought of Senyoreta Eulàlia's paintings.

"Quaint postcard art," I said.

"Postcard art? Maybe you're right. You know how long I've been painting?"

I didn't know of course. But to make him happy I said it must be many years.

"Fifteen!"

He stood and studied his canvas from a distance.

"Fifteen years and some days I feel like they are only daubs. And that young lady—he meant Senyoreta Eulàlia—she doesn't even know how to hold a paintbrush, and I've seen two or three things of hers that have turned my stomach. I wonder how she comes up with it."

I laughed because I thought he was joking.

"Yes. Go ahead and laugh. In your line of work things take care of themselves, don't they?"

He closed his box of paints with the tip of his shoe and he asked me to show him the flowers.

That afternoon I found him in a rage.

"I'll burn her alive. I swear I will. I'll put her on the spit!"

The monkey had opened his box of paints, taken all his colors, and sullied the canvas with a dust cloth.

When I walked over to where the mock oranges were I saw that the trunks of the pittosporums had been smeared with paint. And all over the ground there were traces of paint. They found some on the beach too.

That evening Senyoreta Eulàlia asked me: "Where is she?"

"Who?"

"The monkey."

I said one could never be sure, since she roamed about as she pleased, but most likely she was swinging from some branch, enjoying her peanuts, sleeping and laughing.

At dinnertime, pandemonium broke out. When Miranda was about to carve the chicken in front of them—they liked to see the whole bird—they discovered it was full of sand.

"This is your fault," Senyoret Francesc said to Quima. "You can't just put a chicken in a pan any old way, without first looking to see what's in it."

Quima was very upset. She said the chicken had been free of sand when she put it in the oven, and they shouldn't be yelling at her like that. And while it was true that she had left it on the table unattended for a moment, she hadn't seen one grain of sand, nor had there been any sign of Tití. Toni and I met on the street, and we said maybe it was and maybe it wasn't the monkey. In any event, Tití went missing for two days. After that they tied her up.

But that didn't last long, and the arrival of Senyor Bellom took our minds off the monkey. That was the year he became friends with Senyoret. One day Mariona mentioned he had been coming to play chess every afternoon for a week.

The chess set belonged to Senyor Bellom, a set of ivory pieces, and every day when he left he took them with him. He was living at Can Bergadans. Senyoret and Senyoreta offered him a room in the house, but he declined.

One early morning before the workmen had started their day, I was on the belvedere tending the daisies, seeking to spare myself the ravages of the bees and the fiery sun. Suddenly I heard Senyor Bellom's voice.

"Always working, aren't you?"

"What can one do?"

"I thought I might find the painter."

"Too early."

"He's obsessed with the sea, isn't he? If he was another kind of painter maybe I could help him. How does he intend to make any money?"

I remember the conversation well because as soon as it was over I noticed the rosebush wreckage. We had climbing roses on both sides of the entrance gate. Not the rosebushes with white roses that Senyoret Francesc had me plant in flowerbeds. These rosebushes, which spilled outward from the gate onto the street, gave a lot of roses, but they were poor quality roses. They wilted quickly and the stems couldn't hold them; they weren't stem roses meant for a vase, they were droopy roses meant to adorn a wall. But these rosebushes flowered all year long. They never stopped blooming. They were still hard at work in November. That's what we asked of them. That morning, however, I found the ground strewn with a congeries of blossoms, not one was left on the bushes. I went in search of the monkey, calm and methodical, and I finally found her sunning herself placidly on the belvedere railing. I approached her saying, here pretty little thing, here pretty little thing . . . and the wallop I gave her sent her sailing through the air a full ten meters.

She was ill for a couple of days and no one knew what was troubling her.

The chess games came to an abrupt end the day two of the pieces went missing. It seems the monkey stole them while they were playing. You would think that the world had fallen apart. Senyor Bellom, for all his smiles and bonhomie, wasn't to be trifled with. He immediately said it was Tití who had taken them, he was sure of it because she had sat on his lap for a moment, and it was lunacy to keep such a cunning little beast untethered.

"One of these days something truly regrettable is going to happen. You don't seem to realize what a monkey is capable of."

And he stormed off. Quima said he was in a foul mood because the work on the house was lasting longer than expected.

Then, as if to taunt us all, Senyoreta Maragda, aided by Mariona, made Tití an outfit: plaid trousers, a green blazer, and a little red hat with a very long feather. The day the monkey first wore her new ensemble Mariona came to show me.

"Look how adorable she is."

She had the monkey on a leash, and the animal kept bounding with joy and looking down at her little chest with the six golden buttons, and clapping her hands, wheeling around like a spinning top.

I shook them off as fast as I could. I stopped work midafternoon. I put my tools away and paused for a moment in front of the door to my house, which was standing open, wondering if I had left without closing it. But no. I had closed it all right. I entered, and there was the monkey, in the rocking chair. On rainy days Cecília spent the afternoon there, and I would sit there at night, and she would put on her nightdress and wrap herself in a sort of crocheted wool shawl and come to sit on my lap. I would rock her until she fell asleep and then I would carry her to bed. When I saw the monkey seated in the rocking chair like a lady, staring at me with that insolent look on her face, I almost went wild. She must have noticed, because without my saying a word, she vaulted to the floor and scampered away.

The following day I searched for her constantly, but I couldn't find her. It was as if she had vanished into thin air. And we never saw her again. They all thought someone had killed her, and I did too, but no one knew who it had been. It may sound strange, but I was a little sad about it.

That's how things stood when we received a letter announcing the death of Senyoret Sebastià. It seems he had been tracking some elephant poachers, and when he surprised them, they murdered him and two or three others in his party. When they found them a few days later only three or four pieces remained of their bodies.

Senyoreta Eulàlia fell ill. She kept the last letters from her husband under her pillow and she would read them from time to time. And apparently she wept all the salt from her body.

When they left, Quima and I were standing at the gate.

That was a hard winter. Windy. Rainy. Cold. I tried to store all the plants in the greenhouse and they scarcely fit. I found the two chess pieces beneath one of the magnolias. The wind must have knocked them down from a fork in a branch. There was no sign of Senyor Bellom, and the work on his house had stopped. I killed time by chopping wood and keeping watch on the stove in the greenhouse. Senyoret had promised me he would wire the greenhouse for electricity, but it never seemed to get done.

Toni took care of the horses and devoted his evenings to playing cards in the café. He had become friendly with a girl. Or so they said.

I spent my days alone with my seeds and bulbs, with my things, my eucalyptus. At night the wind was like a voice. Some Sunday afternoons, when Quima brought back my laundry clean and scented, she would stay and keep me company, and we drank hot chocolate together, and she would tell me what was going on in the village.

I stayed in bed many mornings and neglected the garden. That autumn I let the leaves rot rather than burn them. They lay quietly along the paths, where the wind had left them, and with each new rainfall they blended more into the earth. They would nourish the soil and help my spring plants grow.

I never even glanced at the sea. That January was the coldest month of my life. The world seemed to have turned white. Not from snow, but from a kind of frost and a kind of brightness that the sky bestowed on us. On sun-filled days I would sit outside my front door in my low chair and bask in the glow. I would sit quietly, somnolent, and as soon as the sun dropped behind the eucalyptus I would go inside. On rainy days the garden was a field of black tree trunks that extended as far as the eye could see. And the rain enhanced the smell of decay from the dead leaves.

IV

IN FEBRUARY, WITH THE LENGTHENING OF DAYS AND MARCH around the corner, I began to emerge from my torpor. The work-men returned to the villa next door and everything slowly started to come to life. I piled the rotted leaves into heaps and carried them in a wheelbarrow to a spot behind the house. Day after day I turned them deeper into the earth, which slowly became black as night. The sky filled with stars again, and in the evenings you could hear something stirring in the roots. Spring was putting everything back in its place: the rose on the rosebush, the bird in the tree.

Senyoreta Eulàlia was the first to arrive that year. I was glad to see her again. She was thinner. She said she had spent part of the winter abroad and had come before the others because she wanted to make good use of her time until the autumn. She said she was grateful she had her painting, it was all she thought about. Even though she mentioned that the doctor had found a weakness in her heart and that she tired easily, she looked well and seemed to have recovered from her grief.

She hardly ventured outside the house those first few days. But one morning I found her by the mulberry trees in a pensive sort of trance.

"You know what I want to paint?" she said. "Some of those blue flowers, creepers, Saint Joseph's Tears I think they're called. I'd like to put a bouquet of them by the window in your house, the window with the little panes, and paint the whole scene. I don't suppose we have any of them in our garden?"

Of course we did not. They are sticky little flowers, ungainly things. I told her some of Quima's neighbors had some in their courtyard and if she asked them they would give her a bunch.

She seemed pleased. She always was when she talked, but when she was quiet there was such sadness in her eyes.

Mingo came by one Sunday. He was working in a nearby village and was hoping to find Mariona; she hadn't replied to his last letter, but in a previous one she said they would be arriving earlier that year.

Senyoreta Eulàlia told him that Mariona was doing well and that, yes, they were planning to come up soon. Mariona was making good progress with her sewing at Senyoreta Maragda's, and she was growing rather vain because Senyoreta Rosamaria sent both her and Miranda to the hairdresser's every couple of weeks, and when the manicurist came to do Senyoreta's hands, she did the maids' as well.

I saw straight away that Mingo wasn't happy about this. His gaze was dark and he had a worried look. Before he left he wrote Mariona a letter and asked me to give it to her.

They arrived at the beginning of June. The plasterers were already busy at Senyor Bellom's villa, and specialized workmen were laying the bottom of the swimming pool with a mosaic tile that had crabs and starfish of different colors. Stacks of slate for paving the paths lay in piles everywhere.

I gave Mariona the letter as soon as I saw her. She read it in front of me with great attention and folded it up.

"He asks if I want to marry him. What would you do?"

"I'd think about it very carefully."

"I like him, don't think I don't. I'm just not sure I love him enough."

"If you don't know, my child, how do you expect *me* to know?"

"It's just that he's only a laborer."

"Who might become a skilled mason, and even a master mason."

"You think so?"

"Why not?"

As soon as Senyor Bellom's stable was ready, they brought the horses. Everyone went to have a look. One was grey and the other was a light chestnut with darker spots. "Race horses," Toni said. The man who looked after Senyor Bellom's horses was called Guy, and he was half French and half American. He and Toni were not keen on each other. They exchanged compliments, sure, but if Guy took their horses out for a run in the morning, Toni would take ours out in the afternoon. He was green with envy.

"I wouldn't be surprised if these horses of Senyor Bellom's could dance; take a look at their hooves."

And he was right, their hooves seemed to glide along as if there was nothing above them.

The first day Senyor Bellom came calling, he was extremely

happy. I gave him the chess pieces and he offered me a big tip. I wouldn't take it.

"You'll always be poor if you insist on such courtesies."

He could not sit still. He realized the enormous impact his horses had made and he talked of nothing else. "They cost me a fortune, but it's not a problem," he said. His daughter and son-in-law, especially his daughter, were dying to settle into the house. When he was leaving, Senyoret Francesc told him the house was coming together beautifully. They admired it for a while from the gate.

"I don't know what to do with all my money. I spend and spend, but hardly notice it's gone."

Senyoret and Senyoreta had had quite enough of such cheerfulness and ostentation and said Senyor Bellom was a madman who imagined himself rich. Mad or not, he was forging ahead. That same day, however, he was dealt a blow. In midafternoon, a beat-up car arrived with an elderly man and two younger men who addressed Senyor Bellom with great respect. The elderly man wore a wrinkled trench coat, and a beret pulled down over his ears, and though he was getting on in years he wandered about shouting at people and causing quite a ruckus. He was the architect. He had them tear down a wall because the master builder had made a mistake. The whole scene was mayhem.

That was the week Senyoret Francesc and Senyor Bellom took up their chess games again.

I noticed Senyoreta was often alone when she set out on horseback. Some afternoons she rode Fletxa through the linden trees. She looked after him as if he was a son.

"I have an obligation here," Toni said. "Some days I feel like throwing in the towel, but then I see that horse with his shiny coat, and I have to keep going."

He said he was fed up with life. Everything was closing in on him: the village, the winter, the summer, the sea . . . the whole bit. There was no rhyme or reason to anything. And his own son was becoming more and more of a rascal.

"It's not good for children to be shut away at school. Better to have them at home, even if it's a shack . . ."

He had tried to keep his son with him before coming here, he said, but he was often away and the boy was always up to some mischief. He would answer back, practically lived on the street, and he stole watermelons. Not an easy thing to do.

"Maybe if you got married . . ."

He gave a low laugh and said he wasn't willing to support a woman just so she could crowd his bed.

"I like to sleep alone, like a king. I've been married once and I've crossed that one off."

One night I went up to his apartment above the stable and I found him seated with a half-empty wine bottle in front of him. Several times I had suspected he was bending his elbow. He started rambling on again about the same things. The weather, life, the days when he earned a good living with his horses, riding like the devil, and the son who didn't share his passion. He said maybe, while he was off racing, his wife had made the boy with another man. And he started weeping like a baby.

On the eve of Saint John the family hosted a big dinner party. They invited Senyor Bellom. Everyone was dressed to the nines, as if they were strangers to each other. Miranda and Mariona were a vision! Skin-hugging silk dresses the color of ash and high heels to match, seductive little aprons, lace headpieces with black ribbons that fell to the hems of their skirts. Senyor Bellom was a full three sheets to the wind. He kept saying he was prepared to wage war on anyone, and once he had declared victory he would turn his attention to helping his friends, and whoopee and hurrah, and if any of them dared misbehave he was packing them off to cut sugarcane with the black folk. And he said he would like to wind down the party by sleeping with the maids, for he didn't fancy the ladies. He sat down on a plate and carried on pontificating. Then suddenly he sprang up, grasped a crystal decanter, and began pouring wine over his head until there was none left. Senyoret took hold of him and dragged him upstairs, and together with Feliu and a guest whom no one seemed to know, they undressed him and wrestled him into the bathtub. He vomited something awful, and then they rubbed him down with spirits of wine, put him in one of Senyoret's robes, and brought him back downstairs a proper gentleman. He apologized again and again. The joy of being among friends was to blame, he appreciated them all so very much, and it would never happen again. He was like a child.

"If my daughter ever found out . . . she thinks I'm next to God. I want the truth, was I terribly out of line?"

Poor Quima came to see me.

"Two whole days preparing this dinner. Two hours making sauces and watching the roast and choosing the best lettuce leaves. It was all sent back to the kitchen. They had a nibble of this, a mouthful of that. They were all sloshed. Every one of them. Mariona and Miranda only noticed Senyor Bellom because he was up in arms, but the amount they managed to drink would be enough to make the good Lord shudder. The kitchen was full of empty bottles. If I had known, I would have made them an omelette and that would be that! What about you, how was your night?"

"So so."

"Come to the kitchen for a while and have some chicken."

I said I'd be along.

That summer Feliu and Senyoreta Eulàlia were always together. They spent their days on the belvedere. He kept at his seascapes. And she painted strange things. She painted the eucalyptus, but only part of it; she said the whole tree wouldn't fit on her canvas. So it was just a piece of bark, but it looked rather like moss and fog. One day she said she wanted to do the belly of a lizard. And when she painted the sky you almost expected to hear a voice . . . I liked what she did more and more. Without understanding any of it. But there's a feeling one gets . . .

Mariona learned, who knows by what means, that Senyoret Sebastià, when he was in Africa and still alive, had a black woman. Senyoreta Eulàlia was aware of it and had been distraught at first, but then she got used to it. In the end they were like friends, and if they slept together they just slept, almost as if they had a pillow between them. A sword, not a pillow, Senyor Sebastià used to joke. I don't know why he would say that. For a long time whenever the subject of swords came up among friends, Senyoreta Eulàlia turned scarlet. Come to think of it, Mariona must have heard about this through Senyoreta Maragda, the seamstress whom—I can say it now—I never liked.

"Such a nice couple they seemed."

"Never trust appearances."

I was flabbergasted. It was scary how much that girl had grown up. The day she asked me again what I thought she should do about Mingo, I told her she knew better than me.

"You used to stop by the kitchen sometimes for a cup of coffee," Quima said. "Why don't you come anymore? You'd keep me company. As soon as the dishes are washed, the girls always go out for a while."

I showed up a couple of days later. I got spruced up and I made a pretty bouquet of flowers for her, which she immediately put in a vase. The kitchen was a semi-basement. There were two wide and rather tall windows above the sink. The windows were at garden level, and from the kitchen you could see the little grasses trembling. If the girls remembered to put out moist bread there was always a clutch of sparrows fighting over it. Above the cupboard stood a small white radio and a narrow glass filled with parsley. The radio was always on. I would be hard pressed to describe the smell of that kitchen, an aroma with a touch of sugar and butter and hearty stews, a smell that vanished when coffee was made, only to return once the coffee had been drunk. The light streaming in from above made the room cozy. Whenever I walked into that kitchen I always had the feeling I was entering the belly of a swallow. Quima kept it like a parlor. One of her specialties was sole with mushrooms. For a country girl, she could certainly make her way in the world. She had thin legs, a bit knock-kneed, and large breasts, as if they had been placed there by mistake, and a pale round face with ruddy cheeks from hovering over the stove. A face like a nun's, one happy eye, one sad eye. She started making coffee.

"Would you kindly tell me why you didn't come for some chicken the other day?"

I assured her it had slipped my mind.

She lit the stove, put a pot on, and when the water was boiling, she made us a coffee that could revive souls. Dainty little cups and saucers, teaspoons, a sugar bowl: we sipped the coffee slowly, like a couple of ministers.

"Now that we're alone and we can be frank, tell me. Have you heard anything?"

On the radio, a frightful song played on and on.

I locked eyes with her and shook my head, and right away she knew I was telling the truth. A strip of sunshine that had been long and thin when it first filtered in was now fanning out across the saffron tiles.

"You know anything about them? From before they were married? It seems Senyoreta Rosamaria is expecting a visit. That is to say, she's expecting one and she isn't. I don't know if you understand."

I can't say I did. Not even a little.

"We'll see what happens," she said. "I hear she's not getting any sleep. Many nights she's out on her balcony."

"Trust me and stop getting all worked up."

As soon as I spotted Feliu alone I went over to him.

"Have you heard anything?"

"About what?"

"I hear they're expecting a visit."

"Do you believe in ghosts?"

I said I didn't, but word in the village was that sometimes Senyora Pepa could be seen wandering up and down the belvedere.

He turned to me and was about to say something but he changed his mind.

"Come have a look at what I'm painting, and stop fretting."

Senyoreta Eulàlia was on the belvedere in a pair of denim trousers, standing barefoot in front of a painting that looked like it was made of fleece. Very nice. Feliu's on the other hand struck me as sad. Not a mournful kind of sadness but a lethargic sadness. I left right away because I had to sulfur the plants. Aphids were decimating my rosebushes; with the leaves all curled and their underside gnawed at, they were a sorry sight.

I returned later in the day but they were no longer there. They were down below, on a rock, speaking in low tones.

"What Rosamaria should do is love her husband," Feliu said. "He gives her everything she wants and she lives like a princess."

"Are you saying she doesn't love him?"

"How would I know? They should try to get along. Look at them out there!"

The Senyorets and Senyoreta Maragda were swimming far from shore. Only their heads, and small at that, were visible above the water. I leaned over the railing, something I hadn't done since the night I discovered Senyoret Francesc with Miranda. I was very careful. Feliu and Senyoreta Eulàlia had stood up and were strolling side by side, carrying their paints and implements. The waves ebbed and flowed on the sand, back and forth, back and forth . . . whoosh! they foamed and receded, and surged once more . . . and whoosh! foam and recede, now we come and now we go, we lick the sand and rush back to the water, always back to our water, always the waves and their water, water that brings waves but never lets them go, and always the waves pretending to come, summer and winter . . . and here you have these two seashells now . . . and see if you catch us now . . . The three swimmers drew nearer as they glided across the expanse of blue, and when they were closer I started removing dry leaves from the geraniums. I didn't want them to think I was being lazy. She, Senyoreta, was the first to emerge, dripping water, breathing heavily. When she lay down to sunbathe after drying her hair some, her husband and Senyoreta Maragda were still far out.

That night I was sleepless and I ventured out for a stroll. I circled the house on the side of the Senyorets' bedrooms, which faced Senyor Bellom's villa. They, I mean the Senyorets, had the lights on. I sat down on the ground, my back against a linden tree. The light was on for a long time, and finally she came out onto the balcony. I fell asleep without realizing it, and when I woke up the nightingale was singing and she was still standing on the balcony, like a shadow. Quima was right.

On the Feast of the Assumption they all took an excursion. I strolled through the village for a while. For some time, the Excelsior had only been showing old films, ones I had already seen, with lots of story and no action. As I was passing I stopped in to say hello to Bergadans, who was getting fatter by the day. A little glass of anisette at the counter and I was off. I ran into them on the way home.

"Could you tell us the way to the Bohigues residence?"

They were an elderly couple, an old man and an old woman, and they were both dressed in black. He was wearing a hat and she a mantilla. They resembled one another, I noticed immediately, in the way they moved, their choice of words, a kind of fear they had of imposing on others, in how they were quiet and kept their heads down and stared at the ground.

"*Sí* Senyor, come with me."

"Is it very far?"

"Just beyond the bend."

"That's good, because she can't go on much longer. Just imagine, venturing out in this heat when she doesn't even make the trip to the pharmacy next door. Living as we do, in a house with a garden, there's hardly a need for her to move."

"Are you here to see the masters?"

"Yes. We'd like to see both of them. Rosamaria especially."

I said they were out, and they stopped short in the middle of the street and were silent. Just when I was starting to think we were stuck there for good, he said: "See what I told you, we should have written to them."

She looked at me without listening to him.

"Has Rosamaria mentioned anything about Eugeni?" she asked me.

"If Eugeni had been in touch we would know about it," the old man said. He turned to address me. "We would know, don't you think?"

"And if Eugeni hasn't said anything? And if Eugeni hasn't said anything?" she said, desperate.

"Calm down. We'll hear from Eugeni. I'm sure."

"And what if he's changed?"

"He won't have changed *that* much."

"And if we've made this long trip . . . ?"

"You wanted this trip, dear."

I said they should come in and rest, and if they were willing to wait for them, perhaps they would be able to see them.

"What do you think?" he said.

"I think we will, we can wait."

As we were nearing the gate, he stopped for a moment and looked at me.

"Do you know if Eugeni has been here?"

His eyes were beleaguered with a sadness I had never seen in anyone else's eyes. It was almost imperceptible, but I sensed a perennial sorrow.

"No, Senyor. I don't think he has."

"He's our son. We've come to see if Rosamaria has heard from him . . . are you part of the family?"

"No, Senyor. I'm the gardener."

They continued to talk for a while, asking themselves if Eugeni would have gone to see them before Rosamaria.

"Don't you think we should come back another day?"

"You're here now. Better try to see them."

"We wouldn't want to be in your way. A garden is a lot of work. I know because I have one myself."

"You think Rosamaria won't mind being asked if she's heard from Eugeni?"

"My dear, you should have thought about that earlier."

"As far as I'm concerned, you're welcome to wait," I said.

"My wife never stops. I'm guessing you've realized by now."

"Don't believe him for a minute. He might convince you he's right. But he's the stubborn one."

"This is the kind of talk I have to put up with, but you should know that if she had only listened to me, Eugeni would be home now, and we wouldn't be wandering about on trains searching for him like a couple of fools."

"Don't talk so much about Eugeni."

"Isn't he the reason we're here? Aren't you the one who got it into your head to come see Rosamaria? Don't make me laugh!"

"You're tiring the gentleman. Other people's stories are always boring."

"This gentleman knows there's nothing strange about parents looking for their son."

We were at the gate and they hadn't even realized.

"If I hadn't made up my mind to come, we'd be waiting until Judgment Day." She fixed her eyes on me. "My husband, Andreu, is like that, he never knows what it is he wants."

"I'm looking for him too, you know. This gentleman is going to think you're the only one who's searching for him. This is what she does, you see. She wants everything for herself."

"I don't want a thing, and you, sir, are witness to the fact."

"Why must we argue? Please tell me why we have to argue?" He looked very upset.

"You're the one who insists on arguing."

"You made it seem like you were the only one looking for him."

"You just said I was the one who wanted to make this trip. So I am the one who's looking for her son."

"If I hadn't wanted to look for him we'd be at home now. It was just a manner of speaking."

"Do you understand him, sir? If he speaks too much he gets all confused. Just a manner of speaking, he says. If we believed every word we heard . . ."

"Words are heard and they can hurt."

"You see what a hard time he gives me."

"She's the one who goes looking for it. We're here to see if Rosamaria knows anything about Eugeni, and she goes on and on . . ."

I led them through the garden and to the belvedere, so they could wait there. But as soon as they sat down they stood again.

"See that? Look, the Mediterranean," he said. He removed his hat and wiped the inside of it with a handkerchief, then put it back on and pulled it down.

"Rosamaria must be so pleased to live near the sea. She loved the water when she was small! I used to bathe them together, Rosamaria and Eugeni, in a washbasin filled with sun-warmed water."

"She's imagining things now," he whispered to me. Then, raising his voice: "Rosamaria never took a bath in any basin at home."

"How would you know, you were off working."

"We didn't have a basin at home."

"They would splash everywhere . . ." she covered her mouth with her hands, in horror. "And I had to mop up bucketfuls of water. They were so much work. Sometimes I'd put a bit of rue in the water and it would be scented. Rosamaria didn't like the smell, but I did it because it makes you strong. Once I wasn't paying attention and the sprig that went into the water had a caterpillar on it, with lovely colors, black and yellow with silky stripes. You do know what they look like, those caterpillars that feed on rue?"

"She's inventing the whole bit. Don't listen to her."

"There's nothing quite as rude as contradicting someone when they are speaking. Why would I need to invent a story about a caterpillar in a water basin? Tell me why?"

I said she was right, that sort of thing you don't invent.

"The tears that were shed! . . . She was so scared she ran away to the vegetable garden."

"We have a garden, and the bottom half is a vegetable garden," he said.

"And the screams! So I killed the caterpillar and Rosamaria came back and I dressed her. Eugeni, poor dear, was very sad. I gave them both a glass of milk, and then off she went, back home."

"To her aunt's."

"To her aunt's, but we were almost like parents to her."

"You might be boring the gentleman. If she's boring you just tell us."

"We don't like to stand on ceremony," she said. She gazed out at the sea.

"The two of us, we don't like to stand on ceremony."

I reassured them they weren't bothering me.

"Did they take the white car?" she asked.

"No. A plum-colored car."

"You see? He no longer has the white one."

"Francesc likes to change cars often."

Her skin was delicately wrinkled, her cheeks and neck seemed made of cloth. He had a mustache, a little mustache, white like his hair, but his eyebrows were jet black. They sat down again. He was very still, his legs spread apart. His hands, with their short plump fingers, were splayed on his knees. She never stopped fidgeting, touching her neck, fiddling with the gold brooch she wore on her chest, adjusting her mantilla, straightening the folds of her skirt, and wiggling her nose in an odd way: every now and then she would turn up her nose and sniff the air a couple of times like a rabbit.

"Paulina is wild about Rosamaria, that's for sure. We talk about her as if she was still a little girl and she was about to ring the bell so she could come through to the garden and see the flowers."

"Like a daughter. I thought of her as a daughter. Eugeni was our own, but Rosamaria . . . She was like a little church statue; sometimes I would look at her and I wanted to pray, more than when I was at Mass . . ."

"Paulina was very fond of Rosamaria."

"And so were you."

"Not like you were."

"On my saint's day she'd come to wish me a happy day, she would give me a kiss and stay for lunch. She'd spend the afternoon at the house."

"You should have seen Eugeni if we didn't have her stay for supper!"

"Since we had a garden and her aunt did not, we planted a rosebush that was her very own rosebush. You know those little roses that grow in clusters? We baptized it Rosamaria. Little red roses."

"Excelsa, it's called," I said.

"Of course, you're a gardener . . . Excelsa," he said.

"Excelsa. Lots of thorns."

"*Sí* Senyor."

"Would you know if she's alive, her aunt?" she asked and did that thing with her nose.

"I think she is," I said. I figured she must be the lady who lost her dentures.

"And she doesn't live with them?"

"No."

"See? I told you she left the neighborhood saying she was going to live with them, but that it was a lie. If this gentleman here says so then it must be the case."

"Would it be too much trouble to bring us a glass of water?" he said as he removed his hat. "The sea breeze is picking up . . ."

I went to the kitchen. The shutters were half closed. A shaft of dying sun was slowly splintering among the blades of grass and played across the saffron tiles. I picked up a tray, placed three glasses on it, filled a pitcher with water, and took a couple of beers from the icebox.

I carried it all to the belvedere, being careful not to trip. Senyora Paulina was alone.

"Andreu went down to the beach. He saw the stairs and said he wanted to walk on the sand. He's like a boy again. It's all this anguish . . ."

She drank a whole glass of water without breathing and then she leaned over the railing.

"Look at him. He's taken off his shoes and dipped his feet in the sea." And she called to him. "Don't do that, you're all sweaty! Come on up, he's brought us our water. And beer!"

He came back with bright eyes and flushed cheeks, holding his shoes in his hand.

"I don't like what you just did," she said.

"All the blood had gone to my head, and this brought it back down."

"Were you feeling poorly?"

"No, but I feel better now."

I poured him some beer and then poured some for me. Senyora Paulina didn't want any.

"Not now, *gràcies*. Maybe later."

He waited for the foam to settle. In the meantime he stretched out his legs so his feet would dry. They were very white, old and dead.

"They'll dry all by themselves," he said when he noticed I was looking at them.

"And here we wanted to bring Rosamaria a bouquet of flowers . . ."

"And what did I say? When you go to a house with a garden . . ."

"Do they have any children?"

"Not for the moment, no."

"And she was so fond of them," she said. "When she was small she used to say she wanted to get married so she could have children."

"The things you say when you're a child."

"I know she likes children. As soon as she started sewing she made a little dress for Matilde's girl."

"And well I remember," he said.

"Would you mind if I knit?" she asked me.

"No, Senyora, not at all."

"My wife likes to knit."

"It's for Eugeni, you know." And she pulled some yarn and needles from her bag.

"She's knitting for Eugeni."

"I started two years ago."

"She makes him sweaters and socks."

"He likes to change his socks every day," she said without raising her head from her work.

"She started on her first sweater for him thinking that by the time she finished Eugeni would be back."

"And then I knitted another, always with that hope."

"I don't know why. He said he wouldn't be back for five years."

"I always thought he'd get tired of being so far from home."

"When she gets an idea in her head . . . You see, when Eugeni left, she'd sit in her chair for hours on end, staring into space and not doing anything. If we hadn't put food in her mouth and undressed her at bedtime, she would have stayed in that chair forever."

"I don't remember it much, but they said I was like a piece of wood."

"Just like wood. She was only alive because she breathed."

"And I didn't even want to breathe."

"Everything tired her . . . mind if I have some more beer?" said Senyor Andreu. He handed me his glass.

"I'd like some too, just a little, two fingers," she said.

"It won't sit well with you, you aren't used to it."

"It's just that water is so dull . . ."

"Give her a little, but not too much. And no complaining later . . . It's good, this beer." He looked at me. "See how fast she knits?"

"But I have to look at the stitches. I can't do it unless I look."

"Knitting has helped her a lot."

"Sometimes it brings on a headache," I said. "Or so they say."

"Don't believe that. It's a distraction. Just watch her . . . And when she finishes a sweater she's happy. She has a drawer full of them. All for Eugeni. Now she's knitting him socks. None of them for me. Not one. I tell you I've been abandoned."

He pulled a handkerchief from his trouser pocket and he dusted off the soles of his feet and started putting on his shoes.

"See my socks? Just so you know I'm telling the truth: they couldn't be any older could they."

He picked up a clump of earth from one of the flowerbeds and broke it up with his fingers as if wanting to taste the soil through his skin. Then he began spewing nonsense.

"Wonderful strawberries could be grown with this soil. On the way here I spotted some cinerarias. You know they suck up everything they encounter; what they manage to extract from the soil would give you Swiss chards with stalks as white as milk."

"Ours is a tiny garden, but he's wild about it."

"We each have our hobbies. Take you with your knitting."

"He's always on to me about my knitting."

"And you begrudge me my garden."

"It's a crazy sort of garden," she said. "Everything thrives there. Lilacs, mallow, beans."

"Tell him about . . ."

A gust of wind carried off his hat. We both ran after it. As we were returning he said in a low voice: "If you want to make her happy, tell her that her knitting's very even. With everything we've been through with the boy, she's a bit delicate in the head, if you see what I mean." And he put his hat back on.

When I was near her again, I leaned over to watch her working, and I told her the stitches were very neat, they looked like they had been done by machine. She raised her head like a lizard and laughed with a lopsided grin.

"He makes everyone say the same. But it's true; there's not a single stitch here that's any different from the rest. See?" And she tugged on the part she had finished. "You have to keep a steady hand and know how to hold the needles. Practice is not enough. If you hold the needles a little lower or a little higher, you get different stitches."

I didn't know what to talk about, so I asked her: "Do you make all the socks the same color?"

"Yes of course, no need to complicate things. Brown's best. No need to complicate things . . . And your wife, does she knit socks for you?"

"She died many years ago," I said.

"Do you have any children?"

"No, Senyora."

"You see?" he said in an angry voice. "No wife and no children."

"Would you like to see some of the garden?" I said.

"Let me finish this row."

The old man went over to the potted geraniums.

"Oh, don't look at those," I said. "I'll be pulling them up when winter is over and I'll replant them. Geranium cuttings take fast."

"Why don't you plant ivy geraniums?" Senyor Andreu asked.

"The trailing variety? Not a chance."

"Why, because they droop?"

"Precisely. All the flowers would be at the bottom and there'd be nothing at the top. Besides, ivy geraniums are pink, and we need red geraniums here."

"Shouldn't be so set in your ways. Pink is a good color. And there are white and purple ones, too."

"Meteor geraniums, red! And none of those ivies. They won't even do for an arbor. They either climb or ramble, and the leaves go up or down, but they never cover the base of the plant. There's never any life at the base of the plant."

"You're just not used to them. You can't compare the flowers an ivy geranium gives with these here."

"Don't mind him, he always wants to boss people around," she said without raising her eyes from her knitting.

"I never boss anyone around. I just give advice. And the ivy geranium is a fine geranium. Easy to grow."

"Red. Meteor. If I had to change any of them I'd choose a good, healthy geranium, not a sickly geranium. And bright red, with nice juicy leaves."

"You should see my terrace. What would he say, Paulina, if he saw the rooftop terrace at home? All the front railing facing the street, and all the back railing that looks onto the garden, chock-full of spiller plants and pink geraniums."

"You must get tired of trimming them back . . ."

She folded up her work and put it in her bag.

"I'm done, finished the row."

"How many did you do?"

"Not many. Not many at all."

We started up the linden promenade. All the trees were blooming, but the blossoms were beginning to fall. At that time of the year the walk was full of low-flying swallows that shrieked desperately.

"The scent is invigorating. Are these the linden blossoms that are good for one's nerves?"

"These are old trees. The mulberry too. A promenade such as this . . . you won't find very often."

I took them to see the pansies. Five meters long by two meters wide.

"Gracious!"

"I thought it would make a nice end to the promenade."

"It's lovely. Absolutely beautiful."

"So yellow . . . such neat rows."

"Measured out with a string."

Farther along there was a flowerbed of purple pansies that looked like a large cushion.

"What a tremendous amount of work."

They stood enchanted in front of the magnolia trees, enchanted by the buds and the tallowy, upward-facing flowers. And by each of the magnolias, a kingly tree.

"Come see the roses. I've sulfured the rosebushes because we're having some kind of aphid outbreak. Look at the pink of the Carolina rose. Look at those buds. It's almost as if the air was holding back so they won't open so fast. And what about the yellow of the Talisman rose over there. And the blood-red of the Dutch rose that becomes less intense once the flower opens, and turns tomato red. And see those? They are moss roses. The stems are a thick moss . . ."

"We have one of these rosebushes too."

"But what a difference! There's so much air here."

"Yes, there is more air here."

"And look at these Ophelias . . . and had you come in May you would have seen all the lilacs, a forest of them, white, lavender, violet, cardinal red. And double-flowered lilacs, too. You know the one? A single branch is enough to fill a vase. This is my job you see, my only occupation."

After we had seen the roses we walked over to the stable.

"Would you like to see the horses?"

Toni wasn't there. On his days off he was always out and about.

"And what do they do with these animals?"

"You should see how they ride . . . This one belongs to Senyoreta Rosamaria; his name is Fletxa."

"What a life!"

"You have so much air here! We're terrified they're going to build up around us."

"A lot of new houses are going up in our neighborhood."

"Do you know Carrer de Ríos Rosas in Barcelona? In Sant Gervasi. It's a well-known street."

Senyora Paulina was very quiet, and she began to weep.

"Don't cry, dear, don't cry. What will this gentleman think? Let's go outside, come . . . It's stifling in here. Let's take some air. You know why she's weeping? She's thinking our Eugeni would never have been able to give Rosamaria all this . . . let's go outside."

"Of course. Come, come."

"Rosamaria enjoyed sewing and going to Senyora Maragda's workshop," she said as we turned to leave, doing that thing she did with her nose. "She had promised to hire her as seamstress one day."

"Let's not talk about it. Enough. It's over and done."

"The thing is, we're afraid; we won't admit it but we're afraid."

"Fear is eating us alive," he said.

When we were outside, Senyor Andreu asked:

"How much is a horse like that worth?"

"A fortune."

"A fortune?" she said.

"You heard him, Paulina, a fortune."

"We didn't realize Francesc was so wealthy; we knew he was well off, of course, but we didn't think he had quite that much."

"His father used to wear linen suits in the summer and he walked with a cane that had a golden orb on top."

I took them to the back of my house. I had planted chrysanthemums there, for my own pleasure; they bloomed after the masters were back in Barcelona.

"This is honeysuckle, Paulina. Honeysuckle. And up there at the top, pine trees, maritime pines."

"They're like umbrellas. And here we have the greenhouse. They've promised me a new one this year, twice as large. And with electricity."

"And what do you keep in it?"

"Some delicate plants you haven't seen. And my hydrangeas. But some I can't bring inside. They wanted me to plant camellias in the ground and I've had to cover them with a canvas hood."

We wandered a while longer, and when they had seen the nicest things I invited them in, and I asked them if they would like something to eat. They both said no at the same time, but many thanks and how kind of me. I had them sit down and brought out a bottle of muscatel and some wine glasses.

"It won't agree with you," he said.

"Just a thimbleful."

"You've already had the beer."

"Do you think it'll be much longer before they are back?"

"Oh, you know how it is, they're never in any hurry."

"Will we hear them arrive from here?"

"They honk the horn three times."

Senyora Paulina grabbed hold of her husband's arm.

"Three times . . . just like when he came to collect Rosamaria."

In the end I prepared some food for them because I knew what would happen. They would come home late.

"You still have the trip back, and if you leave on the ten-thirty train . . . by the time you get to Barcelona . . ."

I made them a garlic and parsley omelette, with a plate of tomato. I had the tip of a longaniza left and I cut it into thin slices. And lots of bread. I cleared the table of the laundry Quima had brought early that afternoon, I put the plates of food on the oilcloth, and everything went just fine.

Over the course of the meal we began to open up. Senyora Paulina saw the picture of Cecília and asked if that was my wife. I told them my story, briefly. After we finished she brought out the sock from her bag and she started up again. Her husband and I went into the kitchen for a moment, and when we came back we sat down beside her. As soon as we were seated, without raising her head, she said: "Eugeni wanted to kill himself over Rosamaria."

"Don't talk about that. It's water under the bridge; there's no use thinking about that now."

"Andreu doesn't know my son; here you have a father who doesn't know his own son."

She leaned forward, put her work aside, and she said to him, livid: "Why are we here? Is it because it's all water under the bridge, is that why we came? When they looked at that book together . . ." Her voice broke.

"I'm telling you not to bring up these things. That's enough. You see, it's always the same story."

"He thinks about Eugeni more than I do. I know him well. He thinks about him more than I do. They learned to read at the same time, and they used to pore over a history book filled with drawings of wars. And they were already saying they would get married one day. And they would have if Francesc hadn't lived nearby."

"Stop thinking and knit . . . Enough now. Just knit."

"If you knew how many times Rosamaria helped me with the Saturday cleaning and washed the windows on the veranda. They would water the garden together, he with an old bucket and she with a large, green watering can. When they finished they would leave the bucket and the watering can by the laundry."

"Paulina made them water the plants with soapy water from the wash. As if I didn't know how to water my plants."

"It suited you well enough. And you didn't want them to use the wash water, even if soapy water is good for plants."

"It distracted the boy from his studies. And don't think for a moment this bit about watering the garden was only when they were small . . . She's very persistent."

"Rosamaria was still watering our garden when Francesc was coming to collect her in his car. He'd honk three times and we'd hear it from the living room, and then the engine would start up again and we knew Rosamaria and Francesc were off together."

They were quiet for a while. I didn't know what to say. I felt sorry for them. She continued to knit with her head down; he was now standing and gazing out the window.

"It was terrible."

"And she changed a lot. Such a tremendous change, it was hard to believe."

Senyora Paulina was looking at me, eyes wide open.

"Eugeni was like a shadow," he said. "When he came back from doing his military service we hardly recognized him. He had changed even more than she had, and not for the better, just the opposite."

"When we learned Francesc was abroad we breathed a sigh of relief. His father walked by our house every day, never suspecting the grief his son was causing us. He was always dressed in the linen suit he reserved for the warmer months and with that cane of his that had the golden orb . . . he was already having his car follow him in case he tired of walking."

"He didn't last long. He was a real gentleman, but he didn't last long," he said as if speaking to himself.

"While Francesc was abroad, Rosamaria and Eugeni started seeing each other again. She would come to the house sometimes. But when Francesc . . . as soon as Francesc came back we knew it was a lost cause."

"And Eugeni still thought it was nothing serious. All day long he studied in his room on the rooftop, very quiet he was . . ."

"There wasn't a patch of wall without Rosamaria's name on it."

"My wife used to say that if Eugeni had been a fly, he probably would have written her name on the ceiling as well."

"That's not true. He was the one who said that, and I repeated it the following day and he got angry at me. And when I pointed out that he was the first to say it, he said it was a lie."

"Just let her talk."

He had sat back down and was trawling some breadcrumbs across the table with a finger. He seemed far away.

"And then came the day we heard the screams . . ."

"Yes. We ran outside, scared that something bad had happened. A white car was parked in front of Rosamaria's house, with Rosamaria in it. Eugeni had grabbed Francesc by the lapels and was trying to drag him out . . ."

"You should have seen the scuffle, and Francesc was clinging on, and she had covered her face with her hands. The aunt came out on the balcony and shouted at Eugeni to leave Francesc alone. In the end Eugeni heaved him out of the car, with his lapels ripped, and they started fighting in the middle of the street."

"One afternoon Francesc was calling for Rosamaria," he said. "I went out and I asked him not to honk the horn any more, to use some other way of letting her know he was there, because we were afraid something terrible was going to happen at home."

They talked one after the other, taking turns, without looking at me. When one was silent the other waited a moment and then began to speak.

"Eugeni was desperate, and one day he said to me, about Rosamaria: 'She's making a mistake, she doesn't realize it but she's making a mistake. I want to save her because I love her . . . I've loved her from the start, from the very first day, before either of us even knew how to walk.'"

"A few weeks after the fight on the street we found out that Francesc's father had gone to ask for Rosamaria's hand."

"And Eugeni would come into the kitchen sometimes, when I was making lunch, and he'd say: 'See how calm I am?' He pretended to be fine. One day he said to me: 'She's no longer on my mind.' And he went out again. Gaunt and somber, misery eating away at him. She stopped going to the dress shop. We heard the engagement ring was so shiny it hurt your eyes."

"Paulina saw it."

"One day I was alone and the doorbell rang. It was Rosamaria. When I saw her I was nearly ill. 'Don't you recognize me?' 'It's been so long since you've stopped by . . .' I asked her to come in and told her to have a seat, and she said she wouldn't stay long because she didn't want to take up my time. I asked her why she had come. 'I'd like to talk to you.'"

"She told Paulina she wanted to talk about Eugeni and herself."

"That's what she said: about her and Eugeni. And if she had made up her mind to come it was because we were friends; she didn't owe anyone an explanation . . . but we were friends, and she wanted it to be clear that she loved Eugeni only as a brother, and things had gone one way but maybe it would have been better if they had gone another way, and if she didn't stop by more often it was because Eugeni was struggling to accept it . . . she loved us and always would . . . 'I feel bad for Eugeni . . .' I glanced at her ring and she noticed; she blushed and turned the stone around. I said no, no, don't worry, Eugeni was quite happy, and not to worry."

"Paulina says she looked around before she left."

"Yes. She glanced toward the corner where the desk is, and she walked over to it and said: 'All the times Eugeni and I looked at this book together . . . remember?' She asked me, *me*, if I remembered! She ran her hand over it without picking it up, and she said it would be a small wedding, and not to hold it against her if we weren't invited. I saw her out and closed the door."

Without realizing it she had lowered her voice and was speaking very slowly. He too spoke in a low voice.

"But of course, we both went to see them get married, we were neighbors after all and attended the same church. Eugeni had left the house very early and we thought that perhaps he didn't even know about it."

"It seems that when they brought her the bridal bouquet, she was already dressed and standing up so she wouldn't ruin her dress. We left for the Josepets church before they came to get her. We sat in a pew at the back. And we saw her enter on the arm of old Senyor Bohigues, and all the procession. Her aunt was on Francesc's arm."

"The votive candles flickered, there was singing in the choir loft, and the altar was decorated with white roses. The sermon was very long."

"Because it was the Bohigues family."

"We didn't know until that evening that Eugeni had gone to see Rosamaria before she was taken to the church. She was alone with her aunt and three or four girls from the neighborhood. He took her by the arm, gritting his teeth as if he'd lost his mind, and he told her she could marry Francesc if that's what she wanted, but in five years he would come for her, no matter where she was, and she would go with him. And he looked at the others one by one: 'I'll give Francesc five years of Rosamaria's life . . . five years.' And he held up his hand, fingers spread. 'Five!'"

"He came home late that night. We waited up for him and he didn't speak to us."

"That Sunday he played football as usual, but the day I climbed up to the rooftop to clean his study—I only went up there from time to time—I had to steady myself against the wall. He had wrecked everything. The desk and the chair, smashed; the books all shredded; the small bed we'd put there in case he wanted a nap, in tatters; the mattress too, all the wool pulled out. And the floor had these round spots, dark and dry, that looked like blood. On many of the tiles."

They continued to speak in that way of theirs, first one and then the other, as if they were very tired and wanted to help each other. I was starting to get a lump in my throat.

"We went up right away to clean the room, we cleared out everything and furnished it again as it was before: a chair, a desk, bookshelves, a cot. Paulina made a mattress with the same wool."

"Andreu and I painted it nice and white, and covered up Rosamaria's name. A few days later Eugeni appeared in the kitchen as I was cooking supper; his face was green, his eyes sunken, and he said: 'Why did you erase her name?'"

"And he left us."

"He left as if nothing had happened. He said he was going to South America, he wanted to make a future for himself and he couldn't here . . . He left just like that, from one day to the next. 'I'm leaving.' And that's how he went . . . A full year and no news.

And then two. And now it's been almost four . . . We've come today because we thought perhaps she . . ."

"We thought if we hadn't had any news then maybe she would know something. Because we know nothing. And it's been almost four years."

I had been looking at them the whole time and I didn't know what to say.

I took them into my bedroom.

"See all these little packets? The whole table is covered . . . Look. You can read the labels. There's a bit of everything here: white hyacinths, purple hyacinths, twilight hyacinths . . . and these baskets of bulbs . . . see? Tulip bulbs. Over here." I pulled out the board beneath the bed. "All these are pansy seeds . . . wallflower . . . spotted monkeyflower . . . go ahead, read the names. Poppies . . ."

All three of us jumped when we heard the honking of the car.

Night had fallen. I accompanied them to the front door of the villa, which was standing open, and I didn't have to say anything because they recognized each other right away. When Senyora Paulina went to embrace Senyoreta Rosamaria, she shrank back. Senyor Andreu noticed and took Senyora Paulina by the arm and pulled her away. I left. With the garden in darkness and the veranda lit up, they seemed to be very close by, but I couldn't hear what they were saying. I could see their hand gestures, the expressions on their faces. A while later the elderly couple were alone with Senyoreta. The three of them were talking, and from time to time Senyoreta shrugged her shoulders. They must have been there half an hour. Maybe longer. When I saw the couple standing up I hurried to the gate. Senyoret Francesc accompanied them.

"Are you sure you don't want me to drive you? It's five minutes from here to the station."

"I get carsick," she said. "I prefer to walk. We have plenty of time."

Senyoret told them to come again for a visit, but to give them some notice. After he left I waited until he entered the house, and then I followed them. From the back, they were like two figurines. I finally caught up with them and asked if they had any news of Eugeni, and they shook their heads. After my question she had some kind of fit: her hand flew to her chest, and if we hadn't been quick to grab her she would have collapsed and fallen backward to the ground. We took her to Can Bergadans, which was nearby, and laid her out on a bed. Senyor Andreu and I went downstairs for a drink. God knows we needed it.

"If she can rest until it's time for the train it'll do her good," said Senyor Bergadans.

There was no one in the café so Bergadans came to sit with us. I asked him where he had found the sunflower wallpaper that was in the room where we left Senyora Paulina, the same room where I found Senyoret the summer he insisted on living away from home. He said he had changed the wallpaper just two weeks before; he had bought it from Matias's shop in the village.

"You might still find some if you like it."

I said I wanted to paper my dining room, and if Matias still had some I would buy it. Not that it needed to be done, but sunflowers are so cheerful, and I was willing to change the wallpaper even if I had to pay for it myself.

"A flowery wallpaper is always nice," Senyor Andreu said. He had pushed his hat back and his cheeks were rosy again. He was holding the glass of anisette and water in one hand; his fingers looked even plumper through the glass.

"I'll go see Matias tomorrow."

"If the sunflowers are life-size, as you say . . ."

"Didn't you see what they were like?" asked Bergadans, who was gulping cognac like it was water.

"If you want to know the truth, I never notice much of anything," said Senyor Andreu. "If right now, as I'm leaving, this gentleman told me there was a mule behind the counter . . ."

"Hold on, hold on," Bergadans said, putting his glass down and running a finger along the edge of the table. "Listen, what I . . ."

"Sorry . . . but you do know what I mean, no? I mean you could have told me there was anything behind the counter, anything at all. And I would believe you. I'm just not very observant. When I was little the hardest thing for me was knowing how to find streets."

"That's understandable in Barcelona, but here you would have found your way easily enough."

Senyor Andreu had finished his anisette and was spinning his glass on the table.

"Would you like a drop of cognac, while we wait?"

"I'm not in the habit and it might not agree with me."

"Me neither," I said.

"Liquor and me . . . Eugeni and I were alike that way. He never touched it. Smoking on the other hand, yes. He smoked." He sneezed twice. "I hope I didn't catch cold on the beach."

"You went swimming?" Bergadans asked. He poured himself a generous amount of cognac.

"Just stuck my feet in . . . if you're at the seaside . . . you know . . ."

"Would you like something warm? It wouldn't take but a minute."

"No, Senyor, no."

"Why don't you make him a cup of linden tea?" I said. "It's from home. When I pick the blossoms I always give Bergadans a bag. For the winter."

"Ah," said Bergadans. "He gives me a bunch of linden blossoms because he's like that. But I never drink it. My clients, sometimes. If a traveling salesman is feeling poorly . . ."

"It doesn't do any good," Senyor Andreu said. "When we were so caught up in our problems I used to make some for Paulina, and it was no better than giving her warmed-up tap water . . . Would you excuse me? I'm going upstairs for a moment to see if she's resting. I'll be right down. . . . Oh yes! And then I'd like to talk to you about the trailing nasturtium. Remind me."

When Bergadans and I were alone I gave him a quick account of their story. He listened with his mouth open, and since he was a good man, two or three times he said: "Poor devils!"

"If they don't leave until the ten-thirty train, they'll need some supper. You stay too. I can make them a couple of fried eggs with ham. It's on the house."

He poured himself more cognac. I don't know where he put it all. As he was drinking it Senyor Andreu came back down.

"She's sleeping like a log." He looked over at me, all smiles, and he said: "It was bright enough to be able to see, and without turning on the light I got a glimpse of the sunflowers . . ."

Half an hour later he went up to wake her. She was quite lively when she came down. She drank a cup of milk coffee, and when she had almost finished she realized she had left her knitting bag upstairs and I went to fetch it for her. I looked at the sunflowers and found them even lovelier than before.

As soon as Senyor Andreu saw me coming down with the knitting bag, he said: "Senyor Bergadans insists we stay to supper. You'll join us, won't you? I have to warn you that Paulina won't be eating anything. A milk coffee is more than enough for her."

I said if they would have me . . .

"Of course! And allow me to thank you for all of the kindness you've shown us. If you're ever in Barcelona . . ."

Bergadans came from the kitchen with a plate in each hand.

"Here we are! Dinner's served. Don't let it get cold."

Bergadans had never distinguished himself in the kitchen, but anyone can fry an egg, and the ham was good. We ate at a leisurely pace. We were almost done when Senyora Paulina asked her husband: "Have you caught a cold?"

"No. Why?"

"Because the first time you came to check on me I thought I heard you sneeze when you were on the stairs."

"I thought you were asleep."

"No."

"You didn't sleep at all?"

"I dozed off at the end."

Bergadans wouldn't let us pay him. I accompanied them to the station and tried to buy their train tickets, but Senyor Andreu took me by the arm, and no, no, it was out of the question. When the train pulled away they were leaning from the window; they waved a handkerchief at me until they were out of sight.

The following day I found the wallpaper with the sunflowers, the last rolls that were left. Matias said it would suffice because my dining room was small; he was sure there would even be some left over.

While he was tying up the parcel he gave me a wink.

"So, when is Mariona getting married?"

"Who to?"

"The mason."

Someone had mentioned that Matias had been running after Mariona at the beginning of the summer, and I sensed he wanted to speak poorly of her, so I cut him off.

"If I were you I'd ask her mother."

I paid for the wallpaper and left.

Out on the street I had to step aside to let a car pass, but as soon as it was beside me it stopped and Senyor Bellom called to me.

"Where are you going so early with all that wallpaper? Get in . . . don't be shy."

At least a month had passed since I'd seen him because he had been away on business. I was glad to run into him.

"What's the latest?"

"Not much."

I told him the grass seed he had planted in his garden was just beginning to show signs of life, and his sprinklers were like waterfalls.

"I've seen it already, been making the rounds for at least an hour."

When we came to the bend in the road he began to honk the horn like a maniac.

"I'm expecting the kids soon. Any time now. How do you like the house?"

"It's nice."

"What do you mean, nice. It's the best one around!" He lowered his voice, for Senyor Bellom almost always yelled rather than talk. "Me, give me the modern stuff. You put me in a museum and five minutes later I'm snoring. It's not the kind of thing you can come out and say, really. But when I see those horses, and those generals with all their capes, and the ladies so primly seated, and the young folks running around with wings on . . . Who do they take me for? Don't you agree?"

He stopped the car in front of the gate and asked if I wanted to see his garden for a moment. I was feeling lightheaded because I'd had a rough night, so I told him I had work to do but I would stop by another time. He wanted to see the wallpaper. He untied the parcel and pulled out one of the rolls.

"Splendid! A little cheer is in order. Look at the way the world is going. We'll be packed off to the cemetery in no time if we don't watch out . . ."

Then he said they would have a housewarming party soon.

"A crackling good time! Keep in mind that I started out at the very bottom: it was bread and herring for me. And you'll see ambassadors from South America here, and they'll all be playing up to me because they know that one quick phone call from me and it could be their ruin. There's only one thing I lack: my wife. You can't imagine how we loved each other . . ."

His voice broke. I don't know why but I had the feeling he was putting on a bit of a show.

A whole army of gardeners stood in the grounds of the new villa.

They were designing the garden, which would be tended by Josep from the barbershop and his son, who had turned nineteen. I had recommended them. The day after Senyor Bellom asked me to get in his car, a string of trucks began to arrive. Sixty cypresses. They planted them facing the sea. In rows. And not a single rosebush. Groups of shrubs for the lawn; seasonal flowers helter-skelter; and all around the house, for the trellises, Valencian jasmines, the ones with the big flowers. Every afternoon I watched from the belvedere for a spell and I saw the garden take shape. Much too bare. Such a tract of earth and only grass . . . Behind the cypresses they left a strip of more than a hundred meters long by some five meters deep. I mean that it was that long from the first cypress to the last. A strip of good, black soil, covered with fertilizer . . . And then one day I found it planted with bearded irises. The kind of irises that have gauzy leaves and come in every imaginable color. It wasn't what I expected. I was really distressed.

Quima said she had been wanting to see me for days; she hadn't been able to find the right moment, but she needed to talk. I was feeling down and I had no desire to talk.

"So sad, the bit about the elderly couple who were here. What do you make of it all?"

"What do you want me to say?"

"I hear they should have been Senyoreta's in-laws."

"Who told you that?"

"Don't be so disingenuous. You know how fast news travels at the house."

"You seem to be in the mood for a chat . . . but I am not."

"The old couple spent the afternoon with you . . . you must have talked about something. And apparently Bergadans had them at the inn all evening, until it was time for the train."

"They came for a visit."

"No. I heard something different."

"And what would that be?"

"If you insist on keeping quiet, so will I. I'll come by some other time. You seem out of sorts today."

"There comes a point when other people's stories . . ."

I started to say when other people's stories are of no interest to me, but then I thought that down deep Quima was a good woman, and I should be honest.

"Look, if you want we can talk about it another day. But those two elderly people, as you call them, have endured a lot; it's not like when we're discussing Miranda."

She was quiet for a moment, as if thinking about something else. Finally she said: "Very well. As you wish."

And she stalked off.

They planted two or three groups of pepper trees in Senyor Bellom's garden. And laurels and mimosas. When it was all done, the furniture for the house arrived. One morning I spotted Senyor Bellom running across the lawn dodging the sprinklers, a blue slip of paper in his hand.

"Look. They've arrived. A telegram from Barcelona. They'll be here tomorrow!"

And he rushed down to the beach to give everyone the news. That evening he invited them all to dinner at his house and apparently they laughed a lot. He showed them the artwork he had bought, which he said had cost him an arm and a leg. They were by a fellow named Miró, from Tarragona, who painted like a child. It seems he had painted them in Mallorca, but they turned out too small. Senyor Bellom went to see him and had him redo them in the size he wanted. And with oil paint. Miró had been unyielding and silent at first. But with a large dose of patience, Bellom finally managed to convince him. Apparently the paintings were really crazy, and Senyor Bellom roared with laughter when he talked about them. In the end they all went to bed at three in the morning. I heard them jumping over the hedge, their voices on the linden promenade. I got up early to check on the rosebushes, which were beginning to revive and grow leaves that were free of aphids. I worked all morning and filled two large baskets with dry roses and yellowed leaves. Around lunch time Senyor Francesc came to tell me that, in less than a week, someone would be coming to build my new greenhouse. They had promised him it would be ready before autumn, so I could store my plants there. I told him not to be too optimistic, promises never made anyone poor. He pretended to laugh, and before leaving he asked me if I had seen Senyor Bellom's daughter and son-in-law.

"No," I said. "If they've arrived I'm not aware of it. I spent all morning with the rosebushes."

"He said they'd be here around nine."

"Maybe they were tired and are sleeping . . ."

"Maybe."

When he left I went off to make myself some lunch. There was no news that day. Nothing really happened. Only one thing: Miranda went swimming. Senyoreta's balcony that night, deserted. And the nightingale, dead to the world. Stillness everywhere. It occurred to me that if Senyoret Sebastià had been alive and had stopped by to see me, we might have found a way to amuse ourselves with the bearded irises.

At seven in the morning I heard cries. Bellom's girl was riding her horse across the lawn, her father was screaming his lungs out, and the son-in-law was by the pool. From a distance he appeared to be a scrawny fellow, rather like Senyoret Sebastià. Senyor Bellom, in a pair of mandarin-colored shorts and a flowered jacket, looked like he had taken leave of his senses. The girl dismounted and let her horse trample all over the grass. Guy had to go after it. She was in her bathing costume, and she climbed onto the springboard and dived in like a swallow. Her head emerged from the water and she called out to Guy and told him not to put the horses back in the stable because they were going for a ride after their swim. Everything about her spelled youth. And all of a sudden they disappeared, and when they reappeared they were in their riding gear. She looked very svelte.

As soon as they left, Senyoreta Eulàlia and Feliu arrived; they were the first to rise that morning. I told them about the happenings next door.

"The fellow seems nice, and the girl rides bareback."

"Like an Indian," said Senyoreta Eulàlia, malice in her eyes.

"Maybe things will be livelier around here now," Feliu murmured. It was plain to everyone that he had been quite bored for some time.

Senyoreta Eulàlia said with a laugh that it was the best summer she had spent at the house. As we stood there killing time,

Senyor Bellom came out in his mandarin shorts, but instead of the flowered jacket he was wearing a plaid shirt and a cap with a visor. He came forward, jumping over the sprinklers that were left on day and night.

"Careful, don't get wet," Senyoreta Eulàlia said.

"Water is pure joy. And everything dries fast in this sun. What are you artists up to? Have you seen the kids? By the way, you never came to see the paintings." He meant Feliu. "Where did you get to? You must come over, right now."

The three of them headed to the house. As soon as they were inside, the Senyorets appeared with Senyoreta Maragda, who looked very sleepy.

"Senyor Bellom took the artists to see his paintings."

"Have you met the daughter and son-in-law yet?" Senyoreta Maragda asked me. "I don't know what time it was, but their shouts woke me up."

"What's the girl like?" said Senyoret Francesc.

"Well," I said with a laugh. "I don't know much about these things, but she seemed real classy."

"So Senyor Bellom was telling the truth then . . ."

I glimpsed something shiny in a corner on the ground. A knitting needle that Senyora Paulina must have dropped. I picked it up and took it home, and I put it in a drawer in the kitchen. Then I went to take a look at the greenhouse and removed all the things I had left there when I didn't know what to do with them. I cleared it all out for the workers who were coming to build the new greenhouse. Then I heard voices on the belvedere. I headed in that direction, being careful not to draw too near and pretending to be busy with the plants. Senyor Bellom was there with the young people. Feliu, Senyoreta Eulàlia, Senyoreta Maragda and the Senyorets. The whole crew.

A few days of peace followed. The men came to build the greenhouse, and with watching the workers go about their job, chatting with them, and collecting all the withered flowers, I had a grand time. It took them less than three weeks to finish it. I hardly had time to notice what was happening when they were already fitting the glass on the roof. Then a dinner was held to welcome Senyor Bellom's daughter and son-in-law. A formal affair. The girls came and went, to and from the kitchen, dressed to the nines; two hired servers poured the wine, or else stood stiff as boards behind the table.

The month of August was dead and buried and no one had made any mention of leaving. The days rolled by, one after the other, and September eased its way in as sweet as a cluster of grapes. Josep was living with Senyor Bellom now, with his wife and son. He stopped by to thank me for recommending him. He said it was hard to believe, but Senyor Bellom's would-be garden, bare as it was, gave him more work than a proper garden with trees like mine.

"What about the bearded irises?"

"I shudder at the thought of replanting them."

"And what will you do when you have to pull them up later?"

"I'll need a truck to help me move them out and bring them back."

"If I were you, one of these years I'd just forget about planting them."

"Or maybe . . . we'll have to see. . . on that very first day Senyor Bellom said to me: 'Look, you're taking over a garden that's all laid out. Your job is to keep it the way you found it.' So I'm not sure he'd be amenable."

"There's more than one way to do something . . . rein him in."

"What do you mean?"

"Exactly that. Rein him in."

Senyor Bellom suddenly appeared, and when he spotted us he came toward us, dodging the sprinklers, which were only on during the day now.

"I see the two of you are friends. Well done. Josep really appreciates you. Why don't you exchange seeds?"

"I thought you wanted everything to stay as it was."

"You shouldn't take things quite so literally. These bearded irises for instance . . . they seem to multiply. I've already told Josep that I'm going to buy him a book with all the varieties of bearded irises. It's the king of irises, you know."

"The king of irises is actually a kind of lily, the Madonna lily, and don't forget the tiger lily and the crown imperial."

"Sorry. I'm not a flower expert like you. The Madonna lily is a great one, no doubt about it, but the bearded iris has a long flowering season. The Madonna on the other hand . . ."

"Forget about long-term flowering . . ."

"I see. You're the expert on flowers of course," Josep said. He must have noticed I was growing exasperated. "What does the crown imperial look like?"

"You'll learn as you go."

Senyor Bellom laughed and walked away, unperturbed. In the sun, the grass was the same color as the teardrop pendant on

Senyoreta Rosamaria's necklace. I promised myself that the following summer I would fill the garden with gladiolus. Even if they didn't like it.

Quima didn't show up until Sunday afternoon. She looked rather grim. She brought a torte she said we would have for our afternoon snack.

"I guess you've heard."

"No, I haven't."

"You don't know anything?"

"No."

"So you don't know that Senyor Bellom's son-in-law and Senyoreta . . ."

"I don't know a thing."

She didn't believe me and did nothing to hide the fact.

"And you expect me to think Feliu hasn't told you?"

"I'm telling you I don't know anything."

"Before I get started let's make some coffee. I didn't have any after lunch. They drank it all and I didn't feel like making more just for myself."

I lit the alcohol burner. After Cecília died I disconnected the gas because I was scared of dying from poisoning, afraid I would get distracted and forget to switch off the meter before going to bed. In the winter I fired up the wood stove.

I poured her some coffee and did the same for myself. Through the window I could see geraniums in a flowerpot and the tips of a few cypress trees.

"You know who Senyor Bellom's son-in-law is?"

"The husband of Senyor Bellom's daughter."

"Very funny."

She put her coffee cup down on the table, smoothed the oilcloth with her hand, and watching my expression closely, she said: "He's the son of the elderly couple who came to visit."

If someone had tried to draw my blood they wouldn't have found a drop. But I didn't believe her. I didn't want to believe it.

"He's the son of that elderly couple . . . say something. Cat got your tongue?"

"I don't believe it."

"Well it's true. His name is Eugeni. And at one time he was engaged to Senyoreta. It's like in the movies."

"And what do the Senyorets say?"

"Nothing. It never happened. I'm sure Miranda has overheard a lot, but she's keeping mum. I found out through Mariona. If you could have seen the dinner they gave to celebrate the young people's arrival! Senyoreta wore her best dress. And the other lady . . . Maribel, her name is Maribel, in a sequined dress, tight, black, and her hair like a curtain of rain. A diamond the size of a plate, the two of them flaunting themselves. Senyoret was as stiff as an asparagus over dinner . . . So what do you know about the old couple? Maybe they were trying to warn the masters about something . . . so, tell me."

I changed the subject because we had enough trouble as it was.

"Don't you find it strange that it's September and they haven't even mentioned returning to Barcelona?"

"If they weren't enjoying themselves they would have left already."

"Of course."

I couldn't get rid of her until seven o'clock. Three hours blathering on about the same thing. When she left I turned everything over in my head but I couldn't make anything of it.

For a while now Toni and I had made a habit of spending the occasional evening together. He would come to my place one night and then the next time I would go up to his apartment. I don't know what he did on the nights we didn't see each other, but he always came back very late.

The day Quima came to talk to me, he stopped by as well, but he didn't even sit down, he said he had to be somewhere. He was aware of everything.

"I only wanted to warn you there's trouble brewing. There was too much peace and quiet around here. Things are calm now because they're studying how best to approach the matter. Same as with that monkey. Ha! Mark my words: there's trouble on the way."

When he left I set out for the linden promenade to see if walking a bit would help me make heads or tails of the situation. I ran into Feliu, who was alone.

"What on earth is going on?" I said.

"No need to get excited . . ."

"It's just that I spoke with the old couple . . ."

"If you ask me, it's pointless to give too much thought to what goes on in this family. That said, and strictly *entre nous*, this is quite a bombshell, isn't it?"

He knew that Senyoreta and Eugeni had been engaged, at least informally; he had learned it through Senyoreta Maragda, who knew them all from when they lived on Carrer de Ríos Rosas. She knew they had been a couple, and that they had known each other since childhood, and that on the day of the wedding Eugeni had gone to see Senyoreta Rosamaria and said he would come back for her, and on and on.

"And how did she take it?"

"Rosamaria? She'd known for days."

"That Eugeni was married to Senyor Bellom's daughter?"

"It was the photograph Senyor Bellom showed her. Eulàlia told me about it. Rosamaria recognized him at once. It all sounded rather convoluted at first. Apparently Senyor Bellom stuck his foot in it because Eugeni told him that he had been close to the Bohigues family. Eugeni had asked his father-in-law not to mention it because he wanted to surprise Rosamaria. That said, and just between us, Eugeni should be congratulated. I hear he arrived in Cuba without a penny, practically a church-step tramp. And he endured all kinds of hardship until he washed up on Senyor Bellom's plantation. It all started with cutting sugarcane. Or, I should say, making others cut it."

"I think it's rather admirable."

"To marry a rich girl?"

"No. I mean . . ."

"As Maragda says, all's well that ends well. They were both lucky."

The housewarming party fell on the Feast of Our Lady of Mercy, in late September. The weather that day seemed to have been blessed by God. The air sparkled. The fuss and merrymaking commenced midmorning on the beach and by the pool: salt water for some, fresh water for others. Some of them were speaking Spanish, and apparently there were a few guests from England. And two Japanese, a woman and a man, both of them dressed like the rest, in the usual fashion I mean. The ones who were jumping off the diving board looked like lobsters. At lunchtime there was a stampede of cars heading to the nearby villages, to eat paella. They returned in the middle of the afternoon for more of the sea and the swimming pool. And all the sprinklers were on.

Everyone dressed for dinner. Two orchestras came and everyone danced. There was frolicking, shouting, lots of colorful paper lanterns. As soon as night closed in I stood watch by the boxwood hedge, trying my best not to miss a thing. Dinner was served on a multitude of small tables festooned with bouquets of exotic flowers; from afar I couldn't tell if they were real. The swimming pool was lit from within. I had never seen a pool like that before, lit on the inside. Senyoreta Rosamaria sat next to Senyor Bellom, and Senyoret Francesc was at another table next to Maribel. Eugeni was with a gentleman with a bushy blond beard. With all the coming and going of servants I missed a lot. It looked like it was going to be a drawn-out affair, so I sat sideways on the balustrade between two flowerpots; it was sort of like arriving late at the Excelsior and being given the seat with the column in front of it. When the dance started, it was so lovely. They all twirled around the swimming pool that was lit from the inside. Then all the tables were removed except one long one that was for the drinks, and the Japanese couple did a ballroom number, a dance I mean, and everyone stood in a circle around them. And my attention waned.

The fireworks started at one in the morning. Compared to the ones the masters had had and which had seemed so fancy to me at the time . . . these were like something from another world. And whistling and crackling, and a stream of branches surging upward, and multicolored stars, and thunderclaps, and a rain of gold . . . Whizz! Whizz! Whizz! Everything sizzled. A night of blackest black and rockets that set it alight, with shredded flowers and diamond mines sailing through the air. And all the silver of Potosí. And the grass imbibing it all. Taking it all in.

Once the whole charade was over, the peace of nighttime resumed, and with it the music and the whirling dancers, and yours truly had had quite enough and was off to bed.

Midafternoon on the following day Senyoret Francesc came by to see me. He said he needed to ask a favor. Senyor Bellom's garden was worse for wear and extra hands were needed to restore it to order, and if I was amenable . . . I had already heard from Toni that the party had lasted until six in the morning and two couples had fallen into the pool while dancing, and that the guests had gone away happy; a few stayed overnight at Can Bergadans. My job, as usual, would be to fix what a bunch of idlers had ruined.

I headed there straightaway, and that was the first time I saw Eugeni up close. Very tall and lean, with a flat stomach and long legs, a bit stooped, as if self-conscious about his height. Maribel, however, was almost as tall as he was. I approached them, greeted them with a *bon dia*, and introduced myself. He was friendly. She, on the other hand . . . I'm still waiting to hear the sound of her voice. They dived into the swimming pool almost before I was through speaking. They swam like frogs; her hair was loose, and under the water like that it reminded me of seaweed. I walked away slowly and went to find Josep to see if we could determine what the job would entail. Some plants had been trampled, and you didn't need to be a gardener to see they would never recover. A good while later Senyor Bellom came along.

"Heavy losses?"

"See for yourself . . . I've told Josep what he can do to help some of these plants revive."

"Wouldn't it be better to replace them all?"

"We'll see. For now I'll try to salvage what I can."

He didn't seem to be listening. He looked like he had just been pulled from the grave.

"It was quite a party."

"I was watching from over there." I pointed to the hedge.

"And why didn't you come down?"

"The things you say sometimes . . ."

"What does that mean? Even Bergadans would have been here if work hadn't kept him at the café."

"Bergadans maybe, but me, well, no one invited me."

"You're right . . . you must think me a fool." He gave me a pat on the back. "My apologies. It didn't occur to me. But you could have walked right in! It was just across the way . . . I hold you in high esteem. I do."

We worked in the garden for three days, Josep and I and two others, under my direction. We might have dawdled some, it's true. Before I left I told Senyor Bellom he should think about widening the path around the pool, where most of the damage was concentrated. The following season he did just that. When you're right, you're right.

Quima was annoying me.

"What's keeping them here? I have so many clothes to mend, and I haven't been able to do anything all summer . . ."

"Why don't you ask them?"

"I wouldn't dare."

Looking to cheer her up, I said: "Are they still sleeping in separate beds?"

She gave me a nasty look. She thought I was up on everything and she held it against me.

"Now it's me who'd rather not talk about it."

Nobody said anything. Nobody knew anything. They kept to their usual routines, but they went down to the beach less. The days were often overcast and cold. They had a ping-pong table delivered and, when it rained, they spent their afternoons indoors, playing. They went horseback riding some mornings. Toni came by to see me more often than before. Bergadans told me that Toni's affair with the village girl had ended badly. Every now and then he smelled of wine. And he was always in a foul mood.

"They're killing my horses. They don't take them out for days, and then when they do they go crazy and wear them out."

"And why are you telling me? You need to speak to them. What am I supposed to do about it?"

"If I can't unburden myself with you . . ."

The shadows from the trees grew sad and elongated. The afternoons were slowly drained of color. It suited me fine for them to stay longer. Even if I saw little of them, because they rarely passed by my house unless they went to the beach, having them nearby made me feel less alone. But had they not been there it would have suited me just as well. I'm easy to please. Most everything suits me.

Toward the end of their stay, Senyoret Francesc came to take a look at the greenhouse and he asked me what I thought of it. I said I was very pleased, the whole thing was well done and well thought out and just what the plants needed. And it was a relief to be able to turn a knob rather than having to blow on tinder.

"I'm getting old you see . . ."

"Old? You're as healthy as a horse. You'll bury us all."

"You're not serious . . ."

But I was happy to hear him say that. There are some things one is always glad to hear. He was joking of course, but he was warm. He might have been less than perfect, he drank and lazed about, but with me, truth be told, he had always been kind.

I was having lunch when I noticed that someone was jumping over the hedge. It was a strange hour for that. When I realized it was Josep I rushed to shut the door to my bedroom. I locked it and slipped the key into my pocket. I didn't want him rummaging through my seeds. He asked if I could fill up a little bag with linden blossoms for him; he would gather them himself if I preferred, collect the blossoms that had fallen to the ground on their own. I said he could have some, but I would pick them myself. Senyoret Francesc might not like it if he did. And that's how we left it. I would gather them myself. It's fine to do someone a favor, but too much familiarity, especially with certain people . . . no. He would have asked permission that first time, but the following year he would have made himself at home and picked them without asking. Same with the worms. For a while . . . no, much more than a while, it was two or three years in a row . . . the Boix's eldest son would show up at the gate.

"Can I have some leaves for my worms?"

Then all the boys in the village were breeding silk worms; it was like an illness that was going around. And they would come beg at the gate.

"Won't you give us some mulberry leaves for our worms?"

And me: "Here. Here. Here."

In the end they just jumped over the railing and took to the branches with their sticks, and I had to kick them out. That's how things go. You do someone a favor and they take advantage of you.

I was glad when Mariona came to see me. I was washing up. I had just finished my meal.

"Aren't you supposed to be serving lunch?" I said.

"Miranda can handle it. Senyoret is gone. And Senyoreta Maragda left yesterday because it's the start of the season and she can't be away from her workshop. We haven't seen each other for days. . ."

"And who's to blame for that?"

"Go ahead and say it: me! I've had a lot of work."

"So when are you getting married?"

"It will still be a while."

"Where is Mingo these days?"

"He's in Barcelona building a house. On Carrer d'Elisa, in Sant Gervasi."

"Better watch out; we wouldn't want him to find himself another Mariona and leave you an old maid."

"Don't count on it."

"You seem very trusting."

"You should see the letters he writes me!"

"I'm not sure letters are anything to go on. What about Matias?"

"What Matias?"

"As far as I know there's only one of them in the village."

"It's all a bit of a joke, isn't it?"

"To him?"

"No, to you."

"I try to keep things light . . . . And what about the family, what are they up to?"

"I have no idea. But you wouldn't believe how peaceful it is."

"Strange, yes."

"I like. . ."

"Who? Me?"

"You're always teasing. I like the young master from the villa next door. Did you know he'd been engaged to Senyoreta before she married Senyoret Francesc?"

"Hard to believe . . . and that they would both end up here of all places."

"Ha! It's hardly a coincidence. They came up here to be close to the young masters. Senyor Bellom wanted to build a summer house on the coast and he asked Senyoret Eugeni, who was already courting Maribel, what he thought would be a good location. And it was Eugeni who made the decision. He told Maribel that he and Senyoreta Rosamaria were like siblings. So they all keep each other company now. It seems he and Senyoreta hadn't seen each other in almost five years. Apparently they were like blood siblings."

"Didn't you say you didn't know anything about this?"

"I thought Quima had already told you the whole story. It's all been quite a surprise. Have you seen Senyoreta Maribel?"

"And you say it came as a surprise to them?"

"Yes and no. It seems one day Senyor Bellom, the fool he is, showed Senyoreta the picture of the young newlyweds. She didn't say anything; it's just the way she is . . ."

"I hope it's all for the best."

"*Sí*, Senyor."

"And when are you all planning to leave? Are you the one who's been keeping them here so long?"

"Hardly. They've just been dragging their feet."

Before she left I asked her if she was up on her catechism.

"Whatever for?"

"Good grief! So you can get married. Don't you know they'll make you recite it?"

"Not a chance."

"Careful or they'll pin donkey ears on you, all because you wanted to get married."

She was laughing as she left, laughing so hard she didn't even say goodbye.

They left on a rainy day early in October. I helped them put their suitcases in the trunk and on the roof rack. Feliu had his paintings shipped, but Senyoreta Eulàlia took hers with her because they were small. As they were leaving, everyone called out: "See you next year!"

Their presence didn't bother me. I rather liked it when they were there, but as soon as they left I made my way back to my house and climbed into bed. I was tired. When I woke up I went out and splashed about in the garden until nightfall. The light was on in Senyor Bellom's house and the linden trees had lost many leaves in the rain. I went home and sorted through the seeds and the small baskets of bulbs.

Quima came the following day and brought me the keys. She said everything was in order, the gas and electricity meters had been shut off; she only stayed five minutes, out of politeness. Before closing the door, she said: "They've gone to mull things over."

"Who, the family?"

"Yes. They have to digest everything that's been forced on them so they'll be prepared when they arrive next summer."

"You've talked to Toni, then?"

"Toni? What for?"

And without waiting for a reply, she said, "don't waste your breath" and walked off.

I was exhausted. I had a leisurely lunch and took a long nap. The rain beat down on the roof and a single raindrop fell on the windowsill: drip, drip, drip. I slept like a baby.

I woke to diffuse sunlight. The garden was beginning to die, blanketed in the leaves that had been felled by the rain. I spotted Guy brushing Senyor Bellom's horses. A while later, Senyor Bellom appeared behind Guy and the horses and he waved to me. Then he started walking toward me, and I headed for the boxwood hedge. We both got there at the same time.

"They've gone back to Barcelona," I said.

"Yes, I know. They came to tell me. Will you be spending the winter here alone?"

"As always. That's the way they want it. They're not at all like Senyora Pepa, who lived here year-round, or like Senyor Rovira, who shut himself away here when he was feeling old."

"And it doesn't get you down?"

"I'm beginning to get used to it. I'm a man of habit. In winter I do what the plants do . . . I keep nice and quiet."

He said they weren't going anywhere. All three of them liked the house. And the place. And having the sea before them.

"We've decided to stay on, and as far as I'm concerned, as long as the kids are happy . . . I've had so much of everything in life that it suits me fine to sequester myself here for a winter."

Then the young ones emerged in their ridding gear and Eugeni came up to us and held out his hand.

One morning, about eleven o'clock, I was outside near the greenhouse, separating wallflower seeds. I heard footsteps and turned around: it was Eugeni. He greeted me and crouched down in front of me to see what I was doing.

"Saving seeds?"

"How do you know I'm saving seeds?"

"I can tell."

"I could be doing this to throw them out."

"No, you're saving seeds. When I was small I used to remove the kernels from wallflowers to save the seeds. But this mound you have here is something else . . . can I give you a hand?"

Although he was tall and slender, he resembled his mother, who was short and pudgy. The next thing I knew he was sorting wallflower seeds. And all of a sudden, there was his mother, knitting right in front of me. Only one thing was missing, that thing she did with her nose. I was so sure he was about to do it too that without realizing it I found myself holding my breath.

He left at noon. The following day he was back with a little bottle of glue and white paper that he used to make packets resembling large envelopes. He pasted them together with the glue and, when they were dry, he labeled them with his handsome fountain pen the color of milk coffee: "wallflowers." Then he noted the color: "white," "pink," "purple," "crimson." It was better than those cone wrappers. When he had finished he left, and he came back with three large cardboard boxes, the kind used to store dresses, two grey, one red. As he was placing the seed packets inside, he said: "See? This way they're all nicely sorted."

Then he asked me what I was making for lunch.

"*Escudella* stew with rice and a *botifarra* omelette."

"Blood sausage omelette?"

"Yes. Very nice, too. They make really good sausages here in the village. And when it's the season for wild *rovelló* mushrooms I'll grill them together with the sausage. Right here in front of the house. I'll bring out my grill and build a fire pit."

He stood holding the little flask of glue, as if it pained him to leave. At last he set off toward the boxwood, and he called to me from a distance.

"One day I'll ask you to invite me."

It rained again for days. And I didn't stop, not even for half an hour. I tidied the house and moved several seed packets to a different spot. Some were under the bed when they should have been on the table. I organized my drawers, they sorely needed it. One day I took a damp rag to the mirrors, which were clouded and mottled with fly droppings. The one next to the shelf refused to clear up. So

I unhung it and as I was wiping it, flat on the table, I heard a snap. It had cracked. I was inspecting it when someone knocked on the door. It was Eugeni.

"I thought I'd stop by for a visit. I've brought you a bottle of cognac."

"I can't say I'm particularly fond of it."

"Drink it when there's a big chill."

"I have rum when I catch a cold, and even then only with hot water and lemon."

"Then keep it for when I come to visit."

He sat down and his knees were so high they touched the edge of the table. His hands were very thin, with long bony fingers. They looked like some kind of tool. He said very calmly: "You know how I've kept busy these rainy days? I've been milling about your garden."

I was looking over his shoulders, through the window, at the railing on the belvedere and the geraniums. I was thinking I would need to bring in the flowerpots before the first freeze set in. In the meantime, he uncorked the bottle, went into the kitchen to fetch two glasses, and poured cognac into both. He emptied the first with one gulp, then he did the same with the second.

"Here's to you. *Salut.*"

He got in the habit of stopping by every day at some point. He clung to me like a leech. One day, after he had been silent for some time, he asked:

"Are we friends?"

"If you'd like. . ."

"Then we're friends."

He pressed his palms together, rubbed them for a while, and left.

A week after the bit about us being friends, he gave me a burgundy sweater. He said it was too warm for him and he asked me to try it on, to see if it suited me. It was a little long but otherwise it fit like a glove.

When I pruned the trees he would hold the ladder and help me carry the wood behind the house. He helped me saw off the thicker branches that I used to kindle the kitchen stove. Finally I asked:

"Doesn't Senyoreta Maribel mind you spending so much time with me?"

"In this foul weather she gets up at one o'clock."

He stood before the eucalyptus and trained his gaze on it, all the way to the top.

"A fine tree."

"You can say that again."

"How old would you say it is?"

I didn't respond because he was always looking for some kind of explanation. I went inside and he followed me into the house. I wanted him to see my seeds so I headed straight to the bedroom. He had never been in there before. We got down to business. He inspected all the packets, wanted to handle them all.

"Purple swirl . . . bellflower . . . dwarf nasturtium: plant seeds in groups of three . . . passiflora . . . veronica . . . Japanese primrose . . . purple betony . . ."

"Take a look under the bed."

I pulled out the board.

"What a stockpile! But it's a real shambles. I'll have to organize this a little."

"Jack-of-all-trades . . ."

"And then I'll hoe the garden."

"It can't be learned in a day . . . to begin with your hands will be covered with blisters."

"I used to tend the plants . . . when I was a child."

I could never bring myself to tell him that I had met his parents, that they had spent an entire afternoon at my house. For a while I thought he came to visit so that I would tell him about them, but I was wrong. One day I said to him:

"I have a feeling you're one of those people who lives in the past."

He thought about it for a while, looked at me, and said:

"It's hard to say if I do or I don't. Sometimes I think I do, other times, no. I'm rather detached from the past."

Another day when he had stopped by, I don't recall what we were talking about, he said some people had trouble not thinking back to the time when they were children.

And one rainy afternoon he planted himself in front of my window.

"This garden . . ."

"I can tell you like it."

"It's the kind of garden I would have liked to have when I was little. Not knowing then that such a garden could exist."

Sometimes he would run his hand along the trunk of a linden tree.

"What were so many swallows doing here last September?"

And we strolled.

As soon as I saw him walk in with the cat I had my misgivings. It was a small, sickly thing that vomited everything it ate. I told him I didn't want it.

"I'll look after it. It was wandering lost and my wife can't stand cats. Let me keep it in the greenhouse. I'll take care of it."

I said that under those conditions, it would be fine. He took the cat milk every day, and there was always something or other for me as well, to keep me happy. The day we moved the begonias indoors, we were taking a break and he said:

"I've done a bit of everything in life . . . you might not believe it to look at me now. But I've had to do a bit of everything. A sack, even if it weighs fifty kilos, isn't that heavy when it's the first one and you're starving, but by the time you get to number one hundred . . . and you walk down streets filled with a sickening stench, with dogs chasing you and children laughing at you . . . there were moments when I would have given my soul and even my legs for a piece of garden. No one would ever guess it, would they?" And then, glancing at me, he added: "You only live until you're twelve. I have the feeling I haven't grown up at all."

It would soon be Christmas. Like every year, I sent the young masters a Christmas card with a Nativity scene and the Virgin Mary wearing a glittery crown. I was writing it when Eugeni walked in.

"It's cozy in here. What are you doing?"

"It's for the young masters. I send them one every year."

As soon as I had signed the card, he picked it up, blew on it to dry the ink, and turned it over to look at the picture.

"Lovely."

He turned it back over, blew on it some more to dry the still-wet ink in one corner, and handed it to me.

"What would you like for Christmas?"

"I don't know."

"Whatever strikes your fancy, ask away."

"If you put it like that, so directly . . ."

I've always been embarrassed to ask for things. Sometimes, if I needed fertilizer for the garden and I had to ask Senyoret Francesc for the money, a week would go by and I wouldn't know how to approach the matter. But there was something I really wanted.

"I'll give you until tomorrow to think about it, and if tomorrow you can't tell me what you want I'll have to get you any old thing. And if you don't like it, too bad."

The following day I found the cat dead against the wall. The milk and the warmth of the greenhouse hadn't sufficed to cure it. Eugeni buried it at the foot of the eucalyptus; as he was digging the hole I was thinking how sad he must be, and that he wouldn't remember our conversation. Sad or not, when he finished he brought up the gift again and I said there was one thing I would really like, but it seemed too expensive and I didn't dare ask.

"You might be my ruin yet! Go ahead."

He said he was sitting down because he sensed this was going to take a while. I was a strange man, he said. I don't know why but a sadness suddenly came over me. Finally I blurted out that I wanted a small transistor radio because it would keep me company, being alone so much of the time. He replied that my wish was granted, and it wouldn't even be a gift because he would just give me the one he already had. I asked if it happened to be white. I would have preferred for it to be white, like the one they kept in the kitchen, but it turned out to be light grey, not white, and I said that would be fine. He set off to fetch it and came back at once. It worked like a charm. As we were listening to it he tapped me on the shoulder.

"I'd like to have snails for lunch one of these days. With all this rain the fields and roads must be brimming with them."

Early in the morning two days later we went hunting for snails. Our basket was soon full. We wended our way back along the road by the cemetery.

"It's nice, this cemetery."

We went in to look at the crosses. He wanted to see every one of them so I wandered outside and sat on the stone ledge because I'm not really one for graveyards. When he came out he said it was a cemetery with a wonderful view. With the sea in front. And full of lizards and ants. Slowly we made our way down to the village. At the Excelsior they had posters up for a guns-and-horses movie, one of those airy films with trees and rivers and saloon brawls. I thought I'd go see it on Sunday, like a proper gentleman, all alone so no one would disturb me.

I fasted the snails for several days in an old porcelain pot, with the lid on so they wouldn't be taking any excursions, and when they had fasted enough I washed them with water and vinegar. Seven rinses. And into the pot to boil with a bundle of string-tied fennel. I heard him come in as I was preparing the vinaigrette. And as soon as he walked into the kitchen he said he was ravenous. I scarcely had time to drain the snails. I served them with the sauce on the side and a toothpick to pluck them out because some of them had burrowed deep inside their shells. We cleaned our plates, didn't leave a single one. When we had finished we took our plates and tossed the shells into the pail. And then, without thanking me, he said: "I'll be off."

I asked where he was going in such a hurry.

"To lunch; they're expecting me."

I could have killed him. Without even washing up, I dragged my chair outdoors; the sun was out and I needed to shake off my anger. A while later Toni came along.

"Fed up with that scoundrel yet? He's rich, no? So let him chase his own tail. Me, I would have sent him packing long ago."

I started to say he should mind his own business, but I bit my tongue.

"It's no good being too fussy."

I had never wanted to argue with Toni because, on the days when I was feeling lazy or had too much work, he would go down to the village for me and bring me the groceries I needed. And Quima took care of my clothes. It was a good arrangement.

He returned one afternoon, three or four days later. As soon as I saw him I said I couldn't entertain him because I had to air out the big house. I don't know how he managed it, but without asking permission, and without my saying a word, somehow he was standing beside me as I turned the key in the lock. We opened everything up, the ground floor, the top floor, the kitchen . . . and as the air swept through the house we stepped out onto one of the balconies upstairs. We had a clear view of his villa and our garden, everything except my little house and the greenhouse. We stood there for a good while without speaking, just gazing out. When the sun set we started to close up the house. He inspected everything. He opened a drawer.

"Senyoreta Rosamaria wouldn't like that at all."

"I didn't mean to do it."

On Christmas Eve I received the money the masters sent me every year, and a package of *turrón*. As if they had some kind of agreement, Eugeni also brought me some of the same Christmas nougat. And he gave me a banknote. I said it was too much but he made me keep it.

He was away for a few days with Maribel and Senyor Bellom. When he returned, for New Year's, they had guests and I scarcely caught a glimpse of them. That month of January was the doldrums. Toni became a recluse and hardly even glanced at the horses; as for Josep, I had never wanted to have any dealings with him, but even if I had . . . he spent his time in the village making small talk and loafing about. Then one day Eugeni came by to let me know he and Maribel were off to Switzerland. They were going skiing. And they wouldn't be back until mid-February.

"Can I have the key?"

"What key?"

"The key, so I can air out the house."

I was about to say, "We aired it out not too long ago," but when I looked at him I was unable to speak. He stood with his back to the light, with that awkwardness of his about being too tall, eyes sunken, cheeks drawn. I gave him the key. It took him four hours to return it. He walked in, put it on the table, and left. When he was gone I stood and, through the window, I watched him jumping over the hedge. I followed him with my eyes until he was out of sight.

They returned much later than Eugeni had said they would because Maribel had broken a leg skiing. She was mostly recovered, but she still needed a walking cane. The sun was much warmer now and the branches on the trees were showing signs of budding, rather late in the season because the winter had been long and cold. Senyor Bellom had moved to Barcelona more than a month earlier without saying anything. Eugeni came by as soon as they were back to tell me all about the leg incident. I asked him why they went skiing at all. He asked if I knew when the masters were due back.

"Oh, it'll be a while yet. They usually come up for the summer solstice, around the Feast of Saint John."

He asked for the key again, and his habit of airing out the villa turned into an obsession. I kept thinking: what is he doing inside that house? Until one day I decided to find out. He wasn't doing anything. He had thrown everything open and sat smoking on a sofa, in the middle of a deadly draft. I told him I had gone to see if he was still alive, and together we started closing up the house. We went upstairs to Senyoreta's room and we stepped out on the balcony once again. The linden promenade was greening already, and we had a clear view of their house.

As we looked out he asked:

"Do you like our garden?"

"It looks rather bare."

"Even more so from up here."

And I said: "like a monkey's behind," and we both laughed. As we were making our way downstairs I brought up Tití. He never had the chance to see her. I told him about the mischief she was always up to, and the two chess pieces she hid from his father-in-law. He seemed absent, but all of a sudden he asked:

"So what became of Tití?"

"No one knows."

"Are you sure you didn't kill her?"

I swore I had not killed her; far from it, when I was out planting in the garden I always feared her bones might turn up, for I was certain they were there somewhere. From that day on, whenever he came to see me he would always ask: "So, who killed the monkey?" And on three or four occasions he even asked to borrow a hoe to see if he could find her. At first I was sure it was all a joke to him, but one day I saw that his eyes had turned glassy and I was afraid.

In the spring I went to see Matias and I asked him to send me someone to hang the sunflower wallpaper in the living room. Eugeni was upset when he found out; he said he would have done a good job of it himself. Our familiarity had emboldened him and he was constantly nosing about. For my part, as soon as I saw him I'd ask about Maribel, and he would say she was doing fine and would soon be storing away her cane in the attic. Eugeni was the only person who knew where I kept everything in my house: the bedsheets, the towels, the dishes, the teacups, the old suitcase with Cecília's belongings . . . he went through my drawers, he inspected the forks, the teaspoons, the wooden spoon. Sometimes while we conversed, he would grab the wooden spoon and drum lightly on the table. One day he found the knitting needle.

"What's this?"

I said I didn't know. I had always seen it lying around, and would he please put it back where he found it. He said he had started boring a hole in the leg of a lemonwood table and the needle might come in handy to help him finish the job.

I asked him again to put the needle away, it was a keepsake.

"You can always buy one at the notions shop, if you feel the need to drill holes in tables."

He took a look at Cecília's portrait and put the needle back in the drawer.

The new leaves brought with them the flowers and the birds. All day long you could hear the lawnmower crisscrossing Senyor Bellom's garden.

"I'll be spending my summer shaving down the grass, that much is clear," Josep said to me.

He was at his wits' end because, as soon as he managed to get one side nicely shorn, the other side had gone to weeds. He and his son could barely keep up with the work. They solved the problem by buying a new lawnmower and hiring a man from the village who needed extra work on account of a surprise baby.

The living room wallpaper was the work of a day. The place was a mess, but the following morning everything was nice and neat again. Eugeni came by to appraise the results. He pointed out an air bubble that had been left above the window. He was right. Never again did he ask for the key to air out the house. And once again Senyor Bellom fluttered around the garden like a butterfly. As for Maribel, no one saw much of her.

V

THE WHOLE TROUPE ARRIVED IN EARLY JUNE. I put away my radio inside the cupboard because I didn't want people talking. I only brought it out at night, and on cooler evenings I would listen to it with the window shut. Senyoreta Rosamaria, Mariona, and Miranda arrived midmorning by car. The others came by sea again that year, with the fellow who was teaching them to water ski, but they didn't make much of a ruckus. Senyoreta Maragda arrived alone on the afternoon train.

Mariona was changing quickly. She was now a striking, marriageable young woman. She came by to say hello the morning after she arrived; she said Mingo was now a mason and she had a dresser full of linens, but she still needed a few more things and it might be a year before she would marry. And if she was perfectly honest with me, it suited her fine just to be engaged. She said she and Miranda had become close friends, and that even if some people disliked her,

Miranda was a good girl who was homesick for her country; she was learning to sew as well, but she was all thumbs. On the Sundays when Mingo worked odd jobs to help buy furniture for them, she and Miranda took walks together and they always came back with three or four soldiers trailing them. I warned her to be on her guard and not to let Miranda lead her down the wrong path.

"No cause for alarm. It's just that whenever she sees a man she goes crazy, and they can tell. In every other way she's the salt of the earth."

"How did the winter go?"

"So-so."

I wanted her to elaborate but I didn't go about it right. I had already noticed that with Mariona it was better to play dumb and then she would tell you everything. If you asked her directly, she was quiet as a mouse.

That night there was a terrible hailstorm. It felt like it was going to bring down the roof. I rose from my bed in the dark and looked out the window, and I saw chunks of ice the size of pigeon eggs. The storm raged for a long time. It caused a lot of damage. Snapped branches. Shredded flowers. And Senyor Bellom's bearded irises that were at their peak, all ruined, flat as tombstones. When Senyor Bellom saw the destruction, he said no more irises, they should all be pulled up, but I was welcome to whatever could be salvaged. He had small rosebushes planted instead.

If Mariona finally talked it was thanks to Quima. I had scarcely seen her all winter, but one Sunday, shortly before the masters' arrival, I ran into her as I was leaving the Excelsior and I invited her for coffee at Can Bergadans. Quima was pleased. And when she started back to work in the kitchen she suggested I come by for an afternoon snack. So I showed up there a few days later.

She knew all the ups and downs that had taken place in Barcelona, and she calmly related the news. Most of the information came from Mariona, who had witnessed a lot of things and learned even more through Miranda. I assumed both of them had spent their days with their ears glued to the doors. Quima said at first nothing seemed to have changed, everything was the same as always, but little by little people began to notice that Senyoreta Rosamaria was in low spirits. Apparently she had been convinced that Eugeni was wandering the world in the depths of despair thinking only of the day he would come for her. Whether she would have said yes to him or no was something probably even she didn't know. Most likely it would have been a no. But believing Eugeni to be desperately in love with her must have made her feel like a queen. And seeing him happily married was a monumental disappointment.

"Some people always want to complicate things."

Truth be told, I didn't believe the story.

"Are you sure these girls haven't got the wrong end of the stick?"

"Who? Mariona and Miranda? They're craftier than a fox, the pair of them."

Quima said one night the masters had gone to the Liceu Opera House with Feliu and Senyoreta Maragda, and almost as soon as they arrived they exchanged a few words in a low voice and Senyoreta Rosamaria stood up and stormed out alone.

"Feliu caught up with her on the street and accompanied her home. On the way back to the house she told him she didn't want to see her husband ever again."

"And just how did Mariona manage to learn this . . ."

"Don't be naïve . . . she overheard Feliu and Senyoret talking about it later."

Quima had been slicing ham and dry sausage and she set a plate of it in front of me. Then she poured two glasses of wine; she handed me one and kept the other for herself.

"This doesn't get cold, but go ahead and start."

I took a sip and asked: "And how did they patch things up?"

She said she didn't know, but after a few low days Senyoreta had pulled herself together, although she still wasn't her old self. She rose in a terrible mood and was listless all day, everything bothered her. No one could say a word to her without being challenged.

"So finally Senyoret told Feliu he would have a doctor examine her."

I asked Quima where she had bought the ham, it didn't taste like the ham from the village, and she said they had brought it from Barcelona. But she was deep in her story and she kept going.

"One afternoon Senyoreta Rosamaria had a fight with Mariona over who-knows-what, I still haven't been able to figure it out, and Senyoreta went stiff as a poker. They had to put her in bed. The doctor said it was a nervous breakdown and the sooner we came up here the better."

She moved the bottle because it was in the sun.

"And then she started saying that Senyoret wanted to kill her. Rosamaria kept repeating this to Senyoreta Maragda. When he found out about it he was really shaken. One day, in front of Feliu, he asked her if she couldn't see that she was causing everyone pain. She began to weep, and after a while she said she was very ill."

I found myself thinking that maybe the whole story was true, but when so many people are involved in the telling . . .

The outings on horseback resumed. Senyoreta Rosamaria dressed in black from head to toe: pullover, trousers, and boots. Senyoreta Maribel, as if for effect, wore a cloth shirt, untucked, and a wide-brim straw hat of the kind used by reapers. Eugeni's ensemble matched Maribel's. And that's how they traipsed about, some of them pranked out in their best clothes and putting on airs, others looking like gypsies. Fletxa grew somewhat testy. I never said anything to him, but whenever he saw me he would jerk his head and raise his front legs, first one and then the other. Sometimes I gave him a carrot, though Toni had forbidden it.

One morning, bright and early, I went down to the belvedere to water the geraniums: a few cuttings were starting to flower, a vinegar-brown mottling on their round leaves, the flowers redder than fresh blood. Eugeni and Senyoreta Maribel were standing below me on the beach looking like a couple of tramps. The red rowboat was turned upside down and they were repainting it the same color. It had not been used for several years and no one had given it another thought. Eugeni saw me at once.

"You would think we had fallen out . . . won't you come down and give us a hand?"

I said I had a lot of work to do and couldn't join them. As I was turning around I caught a glimpse of Senyoreta Rosamaria coming down the linden promenade. She had wrapped herself in a very large towel.

"Where are you off to so early?"

No one would have suspected she had just been through so much. Not even Quima. She didn't stop.

"I'm going for a swim, while I still have the beach to myself."

I didn't say anything. The instant she placed her foot on the first step her back quivered ever so slightly and I realized she had just seen them. She didn't have time to turn back. She exchanged a few pleasantries with them and asked if she could help, but Maribel, in that Catalan of hers that probably even she was repelled by, said there was no need, they had nearly finished.

And nothing else was said. Senyoreta waded into the water taking slow steps and soon sank all the way in. When she had been swimming for a couple of minutes, Eugeni took off running. He stopped for a moment with the water up to his chest, then swam out as well. He was fast and soon caught up with her. For a long time their heads bobbed together above the water. Senyoreta Maribel, her back to the sea, continued painting. She must have tired of it at some point and gone home. And I returned to my work.

I had just picked up my hoe when Mariona appeared.

"Have you heard the news?"

"What is it?"

"An uncle of Mingo's just died and left him a small house."

"You must be pleased."

"I am. Mingo not so much, he says it's too far away and will only be more work for him."

I didn't care one way or the other about the little house, but she was happy, so I thought it might be the time to get her talking a little. I hadn't stopped thinking about everything Quima had told me.

"Didn't you say the mistress had been sick this winter?"

"My foot."

"What do you mean, my foot?"

"She's fine."

"You don't seem too fond of her."

And she slipped through my fingers like an eel.

"You're always posing questions, so why don't you tell me how your winter was?"

If she thought she was going to get me to sing . . .

"This and that, a finger in every pot."

"You're funny . . . I'll be off to sweep your belvedere now."

I held her up a while longer. I told her I had already swept the belvedere before watering the geraniums, no need to sweep it now.

"Careful or they might make a maid out of you."

"May I offer you a rose?"

"You should give it to me on Sunday. What am I supposed to do with a rose now?"

She went off with her rose and I told her to come for another one on Sunday. I looked out at the sea and they were no longer swimming. It was the last time I saw them together. The others were already making their way down to the beach. They seemed in high spirits.

When the paint dried Eugeni took over the boat. At first he and Maribel would set out together in the early hours under a still-mauvish sky. They would row far out, until the boat was just a black dot on the water. Then he started going out on his own. He looked scrawnier each day, his knees sharper, his cheeks more hollow. He would row slowly and soon he and the red boat would become one, like Senyoreta Rosamaria and her horse.

Sometimes he played chess, but he always lost. The young master and Senyor Bellom were the ones who played the most. Their games were drawn out, they seemed endless. They played outside, and sometimes I watched them from afar as I went about my chores. Senyor Bellom had been sullen since winter. I hardly ever saw him, whereas before he would often seek me out. One afternoon when they had been playing for a long time there was a dustup because of something the young master did. It was starting to get dark and they were all sitting under the magnolia trees. Miranda had been told to take the little table inside and was putting the chess pieces away in their box. I suspect she was drawing things out as much as she could.

Senyor Bellom was talking about his younger years and his dead wife: her hair was like Maribel's, and Maribel had her mother's mannerisms, and the contours of their cheeks were the same in profile. He talked about how he had struggled to get ahead at first. He said he had done a bit of everything, just like his son-in-law.

"It might come as a surprise, but Eugeni worked like a dog," he apparently said. "For a very short time, but like a dog. And then he had the good fortune to run into me."

It seems he spoke in a low voice, unlike before, when he had been screaming as if everyone was deaf. At first, when he was talking about his wife, his voice was sad, but he became increasingly animated. I was at home and I didn't hear or see any of it. I only pieced it together later, bit by bit, some of it from Quima and some I learned from others by feigning disinterest. Some of the details I'm still unsure about.

Maribel wasn't there. But according to Miranda, Eugeni had been sitting on the ground at a remove from the rest, looking sour. Senyor Bellom talked on and on . . . he had liked Eugeni from the beginning because he struck him as a young man who was driven. But if I were to believe Quima, what Senyor Bellom actually said was that Eugeni was starving and looked like "a feral creature." He was from Barcelona too, and Senyor Bellom had liked that. So he sent him to work in the sugarcane fields. It seems there was a kind of fury in his voice as he spoke, and everyone else was silent, as if they had turned to stone. According to Quima, who had it from Miranda of course, Senyor Bellom was quiet for a moment and then, suddenly, he blurted out: "One day I made the mistake of inviting him to dinner and Maribel fell in love with him on the spot."

Brazen as she was, Miranda didn't dare prolong the charade with the chess pieces any longer, and she left. She missed the best part. Quima found out the rest by eavesdropping on a conversation through the kitchen window. It seems that, after telling them the bit about the dinner, Senyor Bellom said that Maribel had a wild streak, and when she got something in her head it was impossible to reason with her.

"Four months I had known him," he said. "That's what I call getting down to business."

At that point, apparently, Senyoret Francesc burst out laughing as if no longer able to contain himself, and Eugeni stood up and slapped him across the face. Senyoret Francesc didn't even blink. Eugeni stormed off toward the linden promenade, and when he was some ways away Rosamaria stood and started after him. And Senyoret, whose cheek was still red, seized her by the arm and dragged her inside the house. In short, it was quite a scene.

Quima was all puffed up with satisfaction. "Something's eating Senyor Bellom. Maybe he's finally put two and two together."

It was looking like we would have a vendetta on our hands, but the following day Senyor Bellom turned up midmorning and spoke with the young master for a while. Mariona overheard the conversation, not because she was eavesdropping, or so she said, but because she was cleaning the living room and they had left the door ajar. Everything went well. Senyor Bellom apologized: without realizing it he had said things he shouldn't have, and he alone was to blame for the scene with his son-in-law. Senyoret said not to worry, the whole matter was of no consequence.

Consequence or no consequence, what finally took my mind off things was what happened with Guy a few days later. I was having my lunch when Toni walked in with a stricken look on his face. He started off by saying he had received a letter from his son's school. They said the boy had run away. They weren't sure how, but they believed he had jumped over the wall in the schoolyard.

"Don't worry," I said. "They'll find him eventually."

"To tell you the truth, I don't care if they do or not. He's been courting trouble for a very long time."

I made the face one does in these circumstances, and since I thought he had said everything he wanted to say, I reached out my arm to open the drawer and get the pruning shears. But he didn't move.

"That's not why I'm here. This morning Miranda told me that Senyoret Francesc wanted to see me urgently. And you know why?"

"No."

"To tell me that I'll need to look after Senyor Bellom's horses for a few days. As well as my own, of course. What do you say to that?"

"What do you expect me to say? Where's Guy in all this?"

"You think he's given me an explanation . . ."

"Something must be up."

"You bet! I was so furious I went straight to Can Bergadans for a drink. And Bergadans himself told me all about it."

I sensed it was going to be a long-winded account, so I went to secure the shutters without saying a word.

"Guy has disappeared with a girl from the village, Josep's son's fiancée."

God knows I never find joy in other people's misfortunes. But here, and I still don't know why, I doubled over with laughter.

"No need to laugh. Josep is delighted. He says his son is too young to waste his time with silly infatuations."

I had always believed Josep to be something of a dimwit, but I never realized the extent of it. The boy must have been crushed, after all.

"We all know how this story ends," Toni said. "Tomorrow or the day after that the girl will turn up in floods of tears and Guy will be off to tend horses in France. I always said he was a scoundrel."

And without rhyme or reason he too started laughing like crazy.

The weather was splendid, and the days drifted by so slow and easy that it seemed like they would never end. But there was little joy. One morning Senyor Bellom was standing by the belvedere talking to Senyoreta Eulàlia. I was on the porch and overheard the whole conversation.

"I'll introduce you two next week. Just show him your work and see if you can reach an agreement. Your paintings are getting better and better."

I had not seen any of Senyoreta Eulàlia's artwork that summer. She painted only in her bedroom and, from what I heard, she invented all of it. The person who was supposed to come the following week was a friend of Senyor Bellom's who wrote for the newspapers. It went well. The friend told Senyoreta Eulàlia that he would organize an exhibition of her work in New York. They went down to Barcelona together and she showed him every canvas she had painted, and he said he would make her a lot of money. This contributed to restoring the peace. The chess games and beach conversations resumed.

"Aren't you a little jealous of Senyoreta Eulàlia?" I asked Feliu the next time I ran into him.

We hardly ever saw each other. The same had happened with him as with Senyor Bellom. All friendly and chummy at first, and barely a thought for me later . . . but the truth is Feliu, like Senyor Bellom, had grown increasingly glum.

He pretended to laugh at my question, but it seemed to be a real effort.

"Not at all. I'm glad someone wants to help her."

"And you? Aren't you painting this year?"

He said he wasn't, this summer he had come to rest.

"When I get back to Barcelona I'll paint a canvas that's six meters wide. It's all ready. It will be the last time I paint the sea. No sand and no sky. Only water."

He said he didn't know what he would do after that. He was a little lost.

"I'll find my way somehow. I'm not thinking about that now."

I was a bit sad for him, I don't know why.

One evening I was on my way back from the garden and I found Eugeni inside my house, sitting in the living room.

"Will you have me to dinner?"

He had two packages with him, one was meat, the other wafers.

"As you like . . . but . . ."

"Say yes."

I looked at him. One side of his mouth quivered.

We dined like kings. He trotted out the bit about Tití and asked when we would eat snails again.

"I still have some of the cognac you brought me," I said.

I set the bottle down on the table. It was still more than half full. When I came out with the steaming coffee pot he held out his cup.

"You and I will flee to America together," he said. "You'll see how well we'll do. We won't tell anyone about it; we'll just take French leave."

"To be honest, I prefer to stay put."

I glanced at the bottle. While I was making coffee he had downed four fingers.

"You know what they're up to now?"

"Who?"

"The two families. The one here and my father-in-law's. You know I have a father-in-law, don't you? Well, my father-in-law is ensconced in one of those cowhide armchairs, made from a cow he personally chose when she was still alive . . . he just pointed as she was trudging by and said: that one. And while he was choosing the passing cow he said bring me a son-in-law so my daughter will be married rather than single. A made-to-order son-in-law for my daughter: not too fat and not too thin. If he's too tall, we'll behead him. If he's too well-larded, we'll saw him down on all sides until he's the right size. If he's too thin, we'll stuff him full of white beans, like a turkey, and keep him in a cage until he fattens up . . . And as for this household . . . well, Francesc is reclining under the magnolia trees, and as he smokes an enormous cigar, he's saying: my wife is my wife, all mine, and I chose one with the perfect skin, the kind of skin that sets off the diamonds I buy for her . . . all the while puffing out enough smoke to nearly choke the poor magnolias, which are in no way at fault . . . And you know what their friends say? A good summer at the Bohigues house is one you muddle through as best you can. And you know what *she* says?"

He was quiet and gulped down some more cognac.

"As long as the dead and buried continue to fatten up our snails . . . You, I wish you luck. Here you are."

He handed me a small coin with a sliver of a moon on one side. He said it was Turkish.

"Don't lose it. It's a lucky token. So, shall we set sail for the Americas? They have everything over there . . . and the plants . . . so many you wouldn't know where to put them. How about it? Are we off then?"

He downed the cognac and without asking permission he walked into my bedroom and lay down on the bed. As I was finishing the washing up I heard him snoring. I climbed to the rooftop. It was the first night that summer that I slept there and the first night that summer that the nightingale sang his song.

It was a dark night. At dawn, cobwebs of mist lay across the expanse of sea. I went down to see what Eugeni was doing and he was gone.

He returned the following day.

"I left rather late yesterday. I came up to say goodnight but you were sleeping so soundly like you were dead . . . And did you know there's a ghost haunting the Bohigueses' balcony?"

He wiped the side of his mouth with his hand.

"Did you hear the nightingale?" he said.

"It's the first night he's been out."

"Do you know where he sings from?"

"Yes. Right here, tucked away in the honeysuckle by the rocks. All my life he's come to the same spot. I mean . . . this must be the grandchild or great-grandchild of the first nightingale I heard, long ago. It passes from father to son . . ."

About a week went by before he returned. He asked if I still had the coin he had given me; it would be terrible if I lost it.

"You know where I sleep?"

"No."

"On my terrace. When I turn off the lights, through the columns I can see all of your garden and all of your villa . . . everything."

I wandered about the garden again for a few nights. Senyoreta spent many long moments on the balcony. She must not have known he was right in front of her, watching her in the dark. One night I stumbled into him. As soon as he saw me he grabbed me by the arm and led me to the belvedere.

"Shh . . . I didn't dare speak before because there was someone on the balcony."

We strolled up and down the linden promenade for a good while without saying anything. We heard the occasional flitting of wings in the foliage.

"They're afraid of us."

"Go to sleep, it's late."

He said he was in the mood for a swim and he went down to the beach. I turned in. I slept fitfully. This was a long time ago, but when I have trouble sleeping I remember the flapping of wings in the trees like it was yesterday, and Eugeni's voice whispering: "They're afraid of us."

I was watching Toni feeding the horses when he announced that his boy was due to arrive any day. They had found him half starved in Barcelona, somewhere in the hills of Montjuïc.

"He's been kicked out of school and my cousin won't have him. So for now, I'll keep him in the village. And to think I'd got my hopes up . . ."

He was still looking after Senyor Bellom's horses. Deep down he was pleased, but he would have sooner died than admit it. I suppose Senyor Bellom had made him a good deal.

I was about to leave when he stopped me.

"Don't you think it would only be natural for Senyoret to let me keep the boy here?" he said. "I'm afraid if I leave him in the village he'll end up making me look bad."

I said he should ask him.

"I saw him not too long ago, but he seemed to be in a bad mood. Do you happen to know the fellow with the skates?"

He was referring to the young man who gave them water skiing lessons. It was the first time in two or three years that he was there. I don't think we had ever spoken before. I recalled the time Senyoret Sebastià and I had played a prank on him and pulled his bed with a rope while he was still in it. He was a quiet fellow, very young, a relative of Senyoreta Maragda; he spent his mornings lying on his back on the beach and his afternoons behind closed doors studying to be a lawyer. The water skiing came only in fits and starts. They soon tired of it.

"Why do you ask?"

"Because this morning he was leading Lucifer away, and I thought he was a hired worker so I told him to keep his hands off my horses. He left without a word and then Senyoret Francesc showed up and asked if I would please not be rude to his friends. So, don't you think it would be better for me to wait?"

I didn't know what to say, so I said yes.

That evening, as I was debating what to make for supper, I found Senyor Bellom standing at my door.

"I wanted to talk to you," he said.

I asked him in. When he saw the wallpaper in the living room he laughed.

"I remember the day you bought this wallpaper. I drove you in my car."

I asked him if he wanted a cup of coffee.

"Coffee? No, no. Thanks. When I was young I used to drink it by the jugful, but now . . . easy does it, Bellom! Have you ever taken a good look at your own shadow? When I was twenty, if the sun pinned my shadow against the wall as I was walking down the street, I'd keep my eyes on it as I walked along, and I'd go: you're

Bellom, you're Bellom, you're Bellom. It's just one of those quirks people have. Now, with coffee, I say: easy does it, Bellom; careful there, Bellom. If I drank your coffee now, to begin with it would ruin my appetite for supper, and then I'd toss and turn all night. I want to be hungry when I eat and sleepy when I go to bed, thank you very much."

He stared at me.

When he was done looking me over he grasped a basket filled with bulbs that had been on a chair and he lowered it to the floor.

"I'll sit down, if you don't mind."

It was an old chair with a rickety leg. I was about to warn him to be careful, but he leaned forward, placed his hands flat on the table and, raising his head, he said:

"I'm worried."

"You?"

"Me. My daughter wants to leave. She says she wants to take a long trip . . . it's madness. This is heaven here. The village is cheerful. The sea couldn't be better if it had been made to measure. We can run down to Barcelona in five minutes, so to speak. And she wants to leave."

"So let her."

He looked at me as if for the first time.

"When it comes to advice . . . let's not beat around the bush. Eugeni doesn't want to move. Eugeni doesn't want to leave. You know what? I think my daughter isn't happy here. She's a nice girl . . . but something's off. At first she was ecstatic: the sea, the horses. There was nothing she didn't like. Listen, strictly in confidence, what's going on with your masters?"

I said it was difficult to explain because it was difficult to understand.

"Yes, yes. I see. But don't hold back. There's some kind of malaise, no? I think everyone has noticed."

"You don't know the family all that well. They're a bit . . . I wouldn't know how to put it. But soon enough Eugeni will want to pack up his suitcase too and he and your daughter will be off in search of distraction. Too much money, when you come down to it . . . and don't be offended. There's no reason to worry, believe me."

"You know you're more discerning than I gave you credit for?"

"When I was small I used to sit in front of flowers and wait for them to open."

He pounded the table two or three times with the palms of his hands.

"Good. Good . . ." And as he was rising he said: "I'm more encouraged. I'm beginning to see things differently. I'll come again when I have more time and we'll sit and chat about it all. Good, you hear me? Excellent."

I walked with him to the belvedere. I had one hand in my pocket, holding the lucky coin Eugeni had given me. He threw one leg over the hedge and, before leaving, he said:

"I see you've planted bearded irises."

"No, they're gladiolus."

We both laughed, even if neither of us felt like it. Maybe it was true that he was beginning to see things differently, but he wasn't entirely convinced. I was.

Toni was waiting for me by my front door.

"What did Senyor Bellom want?"

He must have thought we had gossip to last us the evening.

"The moon," I said.

I didn't even ask him in.

He looked so yellow it was frightening. He walked in like he had been at my house for hours . . . I wouldn't know how to explain it . . . as if, rather than having just shown up, he had merely stepped outside for a moment to check the weather and was coming back inside. The day was dawning and I had just finished dressing. He started nosing about without saying a word. Finally, with his fingers he traced the contours of a sunflower on the wallpaper and said: "Why so quiet?"

I looked at him. He sat down in front of me and moved his chair closer. He took me by the shoulders. I could smell the tobacco on his breath, and I got a whiff of his body odor, a faint smell of fever.

"May I ask a favor of you?"

"Is it something I'm in a position to do?"

"Yes, it's something you can do for me."

He let go of my shoulders, rose from his chair, and with a closed fist he started pounding the palm of his other hand. He turned his back to me.

"I'd like . . ."

He went to the door, glanced outside for a moment, then turned around and came toward me.

"Don't laugh, you hear? That's all I'm asking, for you not to laugh . . . You don't have to answer if you don't want to. You can pretend you didn't hear me. Just don't laugh."

"I won't laugh," I said.

"The trouble is you don't know me."

He grew increasingly agitated and his eyes appeared more sunken. With great effort he managed to say that he wished to speak with Senyoreta, at my place, briefly.

"Only for a moment, just long enough to say a few words."

When I agreed, he embraced me so tightly I felt like I was girdled by a ring of iron. And he started blathering, he talked and talked . . . about the snails, the radio, which I was wrong to keep hidden away. And he laughed for no reason. As he was leaving he slapped me so hard on the back I nearly keeled over.

"Just wanted to see if I could knock you down."

It was three days before he came back. He was a bundle of nerves.

"As soon as she walks in you must leave . . ."

I said I would leave sooner if he preferred; he gave it some thought and said no. It was close to midnight. I lit the alcohol burner and brewed some coffee because I didn't know what else to offer him. Just as I was pouring it into his cup, he said he didn't want any, this after I had told him I was making him coffee and he'd said fine. He sat down in a chair, sometimes with his elbows on his knees and his hands holding his head, and other times with clenched fists resting on his thighs. The slightest rustling of the wind in the leaves made him raise his head as if someone was pulling it from above.

"What time is she coming?"

"Two."

"Two o'clock? It's not even one yet . . ."

"Let's talk," he said.

I told him that Fletxa was delighted whenever I gave him a carrot and that we had become very friendly, though I wasn't really fond of him. He was too proud.

"The only beast I've ever truly been fond of was a lion, a small lion."

I explained that years ago we had kept a lion in a cage, and the lion had taken a swipe at Miranda.

He wasn't listening. He listened only to what was happening outside. I asked him if he wanted us to go out for a moment.

"Yes. But let's not go far."

We went outside and I suggested we stroll along the linden promenade; she would be coming that way, she probably wouldn't dare to come by the greenhouse, because then she would have to walk past the stable and Toni's quarters. He wouldn't hear of it. The night was thick with the scent of honeysuckle. Suddenly he squeezed my arm, and when he released it he said he thought he had seen a shadow. And the nightingale began to sing for all it was worth. It was almost two o'clock.

"She must be on her way down."

He kept checking his watch. He held it to his ear to make sure it was ticking.

"It used to be that when you arranged a time to meet . . . she must be on her way now. You go on and when she leaves I'll come for you. We'll meet on the belvedere."

The only thing that came was three o'clock. Then four. And then the first streamers of dawn were brightening the sky. When he left me at five he looked like he belonged in the cemetery.

I thought he would be back any moment, but he never came again. The summer was drawing to a close, and Senyor Bellom threw another party. I can't really say why. "To maintain friendships," some said. There was a lot of planning. The lawn got a good trimming. They hurried to plant some greenery, for lushness. Josep wandered about with a tome on flowers and plants and spent his nights poring over it with his son. I advised him to throw it away; rather than retiring so late, it would be more useful to rise early and observe real flowers instead.

The Valencian jasmine hadn't stopped blooming since May, pretty white flowers, but the green of the leaves was parched now. They planted bougainvillea, young and plump and full of blooms like sparklers. One of the cypress trees looked unwell, winter hadn't agreed with it. And aphids had already burrowed into the small rosebushes that had been planted where the bearded irises had once been. The day before the party Senyoret Francesc instructed me to cut all our gladiolus and deliver them to Senyor Bellom's house because they were short on flowers. A week earlier, Senyoreta Rosamaria and Senyoreta Eulàlia had gone down to Barcelona and bought themselves new dresses. They said there would be no fireworks because they were expecting a lot of elderly ladies and they didn't want them to be frightened by the blasts. But there would be lots of music for the younger crowd and plenty of alcohol for the gentlemen.

I walked to the gate to watch the cars arrive. A procession of the best models, full of bejeweled ladies and rich men. It pained me to think about the gladiolus and the fate they had met: the whole stretch of garden was ruined. But those who have the money make the rules.

When it looked like the parade had ended I headed for my supper. Later that evening I walked to the belvedere. And as I was watching the dancers below I heard footsteps and nearly fell over. Beside me stood Senyoreta.

"You're not dancing?"

She said she wasn't feeling well, her husband had excused her already.

"Senyor Bellom will understand. With such a crowd, no one will notice . . ."

She gave a little laugh and said she had gone to take a look at the gladiolus before I cut them, and her husband was happy to help Senyor Bellom.

"You must have been upset. They were beautiful."

We were lost in reverie for a while, and finally she said it was too humid for her. She leaned over to gaze at the sea; it was barely visible with all the lights, but it was calm. I said the moon had lulled it to sleep. We went our separate ways. At home I took out the radio, placed it on my nightstand, and entertained myself until one o'clock.

"We're in for some fun today."

It was Mariona, who had gone to sweep the belvedere and had stopped by to say good morning. I was having my breakfast.

"Did something happen last night at the party?"

"I'm not sure. But the red rowboat must have come unmoored in the night. It's in the middle of the sea like an old sabot."

"Did you let them know?"

"Absolutely not. They might get the wrong idea and think I was the one who untied it. Did you hear? Miranda served all night long, and she says the guests left loaded down with gladiolus. They were snatching them right out of the vases. You shouldn't have allowed them to take the flowers."

"I was told to cut every last one. Don't think I'm not sad about it."

Feliu and the water-skier took the motorboat out and went to retrieve the rowboat. They towed it back. It wasn't until evening that word got out that Eugeni was missing. Everyone found a way to mention it. Nobody learned it by chance. Senyoreta Maragda said it was probably some sort of prank and they were likely to bump into him when they were least expecting it. Senyor Bellom was beside himself, pacing back and forth between his villa and ours, and apparently Maribel lay sprawled on her bed, face-down, weeping and weeping.

In the evening they came over to the masters' house so they wouldn't have to be alone.

"If something terrible had happened we would know by now," said Senyor Bellom.

"Stay calm," said Senyoret Francesc. "Maybe he had his fill of the party yesterday and headed to a nearby village. He's probably asleep in some inn right now."

They were all seated in the dining room and Mariona was serving coffee. Senyor Bellom raised a hand to his mouth and slowly pinched his lip.

"If he were asleep in some inn . . . everything would be fine. But the car is in the garage . . . and why do you say he's sleeping in some inn?"

"I don't know."

Later, Mariona told me that Senyoreta Rosamaria was composed.

She overheard her saying to Senyoreta Maragda: "Everyone should do exactly as they please . . . everyone . . . I've learned to make myself numb."

Finally Senyor Bellom, tired of waiting, said they should call the police. But Senyoret was of the opinion that nothing should be done yet and he managed to convince him. He said bad news travels fast. Senyor Bellom kept nodding. Suddenly, he stood up.

"That's no good! No good at all! It's deplorable!"

They made him drink some cognac. His daughter was half asleep in the armchair. Two or three hours later they began to say that maybe it would have been a good idea to alert the police, the situation was becoming alarming. But no one did anything.

Eugeni was found the following day. Not far from there. On the beach. With his face disfigured because the waves had battered him against the rocks all night. Before he was removed I went to look at him, laid out on the sand. I took off my cap and crossed myself. They buried him in the village cemetery, like a Christian, because they said he had died in an accident.

"Do you believe his death was an accident?" Quima said to me. "You don't, do you? Me neither. He swam like a fish."

But the matter was settled, it had been an accident, and he was carried through wild fennel to the cemetery, with a priest and a hoisted cross. Words cannot express the bereavement that settled over Senyor Bellom's house. Nobody saw them for three or four days. But before the week was out Senyor Bellom came looking for me. He was the image of melancholy as he lowered himself into my rocking chair. I didn't dare say a word. He started rocking slowly and continued for half an hour, as if he was not of this world. When he finally spoke, among other things, he said he was scared, and that it wasn't confirmed yet but it seemed that Maribel was pregnant. That's when he started drinking in earnest. Every now and then I would catch a glimpse of Maribel on her way to the cemetery.

The masters left for Barcelona and Senyoreta Eulàlia for New York and her exhibition. Before leaving, Senyoret Francesc came to see me and instructed me to smash the red rowboat to pieces and burn it.

It was a mild winter. Toni kept the boy at home because he had finally summoned the courage to ask permission. I didn't like him one bit, he was the kind of boy who always looked like he was ready to stab you in the back. One Sunday when Quima delivered my laundry, she told me Senyor Bellom was sometimes seen stumbling through town, and it was a crying shame. She said he was getting drunk at Can Bergadans. After giving it much thought, I paid a visit to Bergadans and told him to ease up.

"What do you mean, ease up?"

I said I meant that when he noticed that the alcohol was going to Senyor Bellom's head he should refuse to serve him. But Bergadans, not without reason, replied: "That would be meddling in his private affairs. And in the end, Senyor Bellom is Senyor Bellom. Would you dare tell him you wouldn't serve him anymore? I wouldn't. If he doesn't drink here he'll drink at home, and that would be worse. Here, at least, he can have some fun."

Sometimes I would pretend to be busy in the village, and I would wait for him to leave Can Bergadans and see him home. He allowed himself to be ferried like a child and we got along swimmingly. He listened to everything I said. One evening, when he was about to enter his house, he took my hand and said, "I'm all alone." He left with his head down. I had a heavy heart, and one day when his mood was lighter I asked him:

"Do you know if Eugeni went to see his parents when he was here?"

He gave me a surprised look.

"His parents? Where are his parents?"

I said they had been here the previous summer, shortly before he and Maribel arrived, and they had spent the afternoon with me because the masters weren't at home. They wanted to speak with Senyoreta Rosamaria because they hadn't heard from their son.

"Remember the day I bought the wallpaper with the sunflowers? They came the day before that, on the August Feast of the Assumption."

We were standing by the iron gate to his house and he asked me to come in. The garden looked shabby and I thought that perhaps Josep was being lazy. He led me to a very large room with one side entirely taken up by windows that faced the sea. He didn't say anything for a while, he paced up and down. In just a short lapse of time he had been transformed; his face had progressively reddened and his eyes gleamed darkly beneath his furrowed brow.

All of a sudden he started to speak.

"It's funny . . . Eugeni and I were poles apart, but he resembled me in some ways. Not many, but still . . . I think of him and I picture myself as a young man. A lesser version of course, because I was known to bite. And hard. I left home too, though not over some silly business like he did . . . I know the story all too well . . . people can't hold their tongues you know . . . I ended up in Argentina. My mother was widowed at a very young age and had to go into service, so she sent me off to be an apprentice to a baker. Things might have gone differently if she hadn't married again. Maybe now I'd have a bakery in Barcelona, in Gràcia perhaps."

He was heaving, slowly, almost gasping for air. Sometimes his words struggled to get out. He stood motionless in front of the windows and looked out at the sea. As if I wasn't there.

"But she married a beast of a shopkeeper and they took me out of the bakery and put me to work in the store. My days were spent delivering boxes of food, unloading sacks of beans and potatoes, eating little and sleeping less, and getting my fair share of beatings. Until I'd had enough, and Mother too."

I couldn't understand what was the matter with him, or why he was telling me all this. If Quima could hear him, I thought. It was distressing to watch. It was as if he was talking to himself and I was eavesdropping from behind a closed door.

"It was my mother who told me to leave. She said anywhere would be better than home. He wouldn't hear of it, and the arguments lasted a long time, with rows and clashes and bad moments, but finally he said suit yourselves; he even recommended me to some Catalan friends of his who had a dairy in Buenos Aires. When I arrived with my bundle on my back and three pesetas in my pocket, only God could say where those Catalans had got to. I found myself alone, with my bundle and my three pesetas, standing in the middle of the street, under a lamppost. And I better not tell you how I got out of that bind. I wound up on a hacienda where they kept lots of horses. Mucking out stables. What do you say to that?"

He turned around when I was least expecting it and came straight toward me.

"Sit."

I sat down in an armchair; it was light brown with a large white spot on the backrest. "The spot the cow had," I thought. He stood in front of me.

"You know why I like you?" he said.

"It comes from the first time I saw you. You won't even remember. It was years ago, when I was searching for a piece of land to build the summer house. Eugeni said I should buy here because some friends of his lived in the area. The day I came up to look at properties you were standing by the gate examining some flowers. It took you a long time to realize I was right beside you. You were so engrossed in your flowers that I immediately thought: this is a good man."

I recalled the day we met perfectly. But I didn't say anything. He took to pacing the floor again.

"I'm not like you. I couldn't have served rich folks for long. I would have set the house on fire or God knows what else. Around here people think I'm too soft . . . There was a black girl in the kitchen where we prepared the mess for the workers on the hacienda. Her name was Lilit. We became involved. She had a saintly goodness and I fell head over heels in love with her. Quite a story, eh? She was trampled to death by a horse. I was heartbroken, and for a long time I lived only for my work. There was a little girl in the house, the master's daughter, very pretty, who was learning to sing and play the piano. Her father was a formidable man. Tall like a Saint Paul. He had made his fortune by brute force. As a young man he had been quick with his knife. Soon he moved me out of the stables and sent me off to pasture the horses. I don't know why but he took a liking to me. Many times I've thought he had already decided then to marry me off to his daughter. And meanwhile she continued to grow; she was sweet as pie and always had a white satin bow in her hair. I was well built and easy on the eyes. Finally her father, probably hoping to move things along, asked me if I would accompany her when she went out riding. I said I'd be happy to. And soon I found myself married to her. It took me longer than it did Eugeni, and it was all for nothing. When her father died it turned out he had a mountain of debt. So I made off for Cuba with what I could swindle from the creditors."

I didn't dare to breathe. I feared grief and drinking had disturbed him. Suddenly I felt an urge to flee. He paused near the door, as if debating what to do, and then he came back, dragging an armchair with him.

"I spent an entire night pondering whether I should leave her in Argentina. Without telling her of course. And I still don't know why, but I took her with me. She no longer wore ribbons in her hair or made visitors yawn with her piano playing. She slept with every known friend and acquaintance. I have put on quite an act, gushing about her later! And here's the best part: her name was Zoila. Once in Cuba I wasted no time. I bent many people to my will and soon I made my fortune. Maribel was a long time coming. Senyora Bellom, who wasn't in her prime by then and had stiff bones, died in childbirth. And you would never believe it, but I cried like a baby."

He squeezed his lip several times with a steady hand and added:

"Maribel is the apple of my eye. I let her marry Eugeni because I understood that, if I said no, I'd be the one to lose out. Eugeni! I took to him at first. But later . . . the times I could have wrung his neck had it not been for her . . ."

It was getting late. And if someone had stuck me with a needle they wouldn't have found a drop of blood. Suddenly he seemed to perk up.

"Why am I telling you all this?"

I was about to blurt something out, but he cut me off.

"Ah yes, because of what I was saying about my parents. My mother is dead. When the news finally reached me she had been gone for ten years. If you were to ask me why I never wrote to her I wouldn't know what to tell you. The mysteries of life. But I swear I loved her very much."

He rose.

"You know what? I think I would like to do something for Eugeni's parents. I hear they are poor. You must know where they live."

I said someone had given me the name of their street, and with the name of the street it wouldn't be hard to find them.

"If I were to ask you, would you go see them on my behalf?"

I said I would. He took me by the arm and accompanied me to the door.

"You'd better go; it's late. I'll stop by tomorrow and we can go over the details."

As I was leaving I glanced at the paintings with the childlike figures and it almost broke me.

He came the following day, in the evening, and he caught me with the radio turned on.

"That transistor belonged to Eugeni."

"He gave it to me."

"Did you know it was the very first thing he bought in America?

I realize you and Eugeni were friends. I'm not on another planet, you know. Here."

He placed a fat envelope on the table.

"For now you can give them this money. Tell them I'll send some every month."

He asked me how I intended to get to Barcelona. I said I would catch the first train.

"Take my car. Toni will drive you."

When we got to Carrer de Ríos Rosas, their street, we decided to start with the lower numbers. Halfway up the street, a woman loaded down with baskets pointed us to the house. I got out of the car and instructed Toni to go off on his own and come back to collect me two hours later.

It was a narrow, one-story house, with a little spike-tipped gate in front of a wooden door. There was a window on both sides, and the sills had flowerpots with ivy geraniums and dusty asparagus ferns. The paint on the walls was discolored, the stucco bulged here and there, the burst blisters revealing the naked brick beneath.

I rang the doorbell. It was a while before someone answered. Suddenly the door cracked and, through the gap, I heard Senyor Andreu's voice.

"How can I help you?"

He hadn't recognized me. I said I was the gardener for the Bohigues family. Then the door swung open and I got a better look at him. He was holding a bunch of keys in his hand and was having trouble finding the one to the gate.

"Just a moment please, give me a moment . . . these keys . . . the one you need is always the one that wants to hide."

He finally managed to open the gate and he asked me to come in. He was all kind words. In the entryway there was an umbrella stand of blackened brass with a clouded mirror. It reminded me of the one we had at home when I was little and I still had the cross on the roof of my mouth. We walked through a narrow hall that had a few loose tiles.

"Paulina! Paulina! This is marvelous . . . from the Bohigueses . . . a visit."

A rotund woman was seated next to Senyora Paulina, and as soon as she saw me she stood up to leave. Senyor Andreu accompanied her to the door and returned immediately.

"We have thought a lot about you. And about your garden . . . what an afternoon that was! And about all the trouble we caused Senyor Bergadans."

The dining room table was round. A cabinet by the wall, with wooden doors at the bottom and glass doors at the top, gave off a scent of spices.

"How is Bergadans?"

I said Bergadans was well, and though it wasn't true, I told them he sent his compliments. Senyor Andreu asked after Senyoreta Rosamaria. Senyora Paulina didn't open her mouth. I told them the family had had a good summer, and the garden had ended the season with an astounding profusion of flowers.

Senyora Paulina raised her head.

"He's coming down," she said.

There was a hush. Someone was making his way down the stairs.

"Don't mention the wiring you had to repair. Just ignore it."

"Senyor Maurici!" Senyor Andreu called out. "Senyor Maurici!"

Into the living room came a man of over fifty, neither short nor tall, clean-shaven, with hair so black it looked like it had been dyed or he was wearing a wig. He was neatly dressed: pressed trousers, a double-breasted sports jacket, the whole ensemble a pale shade of grey, with stain-mottled lapels. And a cane. A cane of dark wood with a worn tip.

When Senyor Andreu noticed Senyor Maurici eyeing me, he rubbed his hands together and said: "This is the man with the garden, remember we talked about him?"

To me he said: "May I introduce Senyor Maurici."

We shook hands, but Senyor Maurici was looking at Senyora Paulina.

"The candles I keep in my night stand. I counted them," he said. "I have it all noted down here." He patted his jacket pocket.

"Don't give it another thought," said Senyor Andreu before changing the subject. "Senyor Maurici is a great artist," he said.

"I'm just telling you so you'll know," Senyor Maurici said.

"No need to worry."

He tapped the tip of his cane on the floor a couple of times and made as if to leave. Senyor Andreu stopped him.

"You know what would be nice? For this gentleman to see for himself one of your tricks." He turned to me and said: "It might come as a surprise, but he's in high demand as a sleight-of-hand performer. If you're not running late, Senyor Maurici, we would like to see one. Wouldn't we, Paulina?"

Senyora Paulina said nothing. She remained seated by the glass door, erect and stone-faced.

"It's getting late . . . but I suppose I could do the one with the handkerchiefs."

"No," Senyor Andreu said. "It's nice enough, but many people can do it." He laughed and looked at me. "He puts red silk handkerchiefs into one ear and slowly pulls them out of the other, as many as you want." Then he addressed Senyor Maurici and requested the number with the ring and the cane.

Senyor Maurici took off his wedding band and handed it to me.

"Take a good look at it. It's gold, not broken anywhere."

He held out the cane, the tip end facing me.

"Slide the ring onto the tip. Do you have a clean handkerchief on you?"

I gave him my handkerchief and he had me hold the walking stick by the tip.

"Now pay attention. The ring can't move in my direction because the cane is too wide. If it goes anywhere it has to be on your end. Senyor Andreu, would you mind unfolding the handkerchief and placing it over the ring?"

Senyor Andreu spread out the handkerchief according to Senyor Maurici's instructions. A moment later Senyor Andreu said I could remove it. The ring had disappeared.

"Well?"

The next thing I knew, Senyor Maurici was standing right beside me. He reached for my ear with a worried expression on his face and said: "We're going to have to keep an eye on you . . . Senyor Andreu, we need to watch this man closely. Look where he had put my wedding band."

And he brought out the ring from behind my ear.

That's when Senyora Paulina stepped in.

"Don't you think you might be too old for this?"

Senyor Maurici hurriedly said goodbye and left.

"You shouldn't have said anything, dear."

She did that thing with her nose.

"Maybe you should show people around the house, and keep it at that." She stared at me. "My husband likes to pay Senyor Maurici compliments, when what we should do is throw him out today."

"Don't pay her any mind; she always exaggerates."

"I'm not exaggerating at all. It would take too long to explain . . . but among the many calamities this man inflicts on us, there's one that stands out: he likes to cut our electric wires at night. We rented him two rooms, the ones in the front. He has two balconies onto the street. And meanwhile we stay in the back."

"We kept the ones in the back because they get more sunlight, remember? The front rooms are ice-cold, he complained about it a lot at first."

"He has two balconies onto the street. And he pays less for them than he would anywhere else because my husband is a gracious man."

"She'll have you believe Senyor Maurici is taking advantage of us. We've raised his rent twice already."

"And each time he's been enraged by it, and each time he's devised new ways to torment us. One day I admonished him for using too much electricity. You see, he comes home late from his theater outings and doesn't mind taking a good long hour to get himself into bed. He goes over his tricks and irons his trousers at two in the morning. He has an entire room filled with his contraptions, and it's a mess. So one day I just turned off the electric meter. I heard him tiptoeing upstairs, stumbling as he went. But the following day he must have realized, and before heading up he turned the electricity back on.

"He couldn't very well climb into bed in the dark . . ."

"I had bought him a candle."

"No, I did. I bought him the candle."

"I told him I was turning off the electricity at ten o'clock every night and he was not to turn it back on."

"Then she started grumbling about the candles, so now he buys them himself."

"I had Andreu go to the company to request permission to have a box made for the meter, so we could lock it with a key. Fortunately the clerk there is a friend. We had the box made and Senyor Maurici was no longer able to perform his nightly sleight-of-hand. And since then, every now and then he cuts our lines. When he thinks we are fast asleep, he comes out of his bedroom and . . ."

Senyor Andreu took me by the arm.

"Come with me, I'll show you my plants."

He opened the glass door and we went outside.

"Don't believe a word she says." He squeezed my arm. "It's best just to ignore her. She's the one who cuts the power lines. Everything was about Senyor Maurici before. She gushed about him nonstop, sunup to sundown, to anyone who would listen . . . we didn't deserve our luck, such a respectful man who never made a nuisance of himself. She had a one-hundred watt bulb installed for him. And suddenly the praise ended. Now she can't abide him. You've seen for yourself: he's a peaceful man. So in order to turn me against him she started cutting the power lines. She climbs up on chairs and tables. I'm a light sleeper, and I always hear her when she's heading out on her rampage. She's going to break her neck one of these days. She wants me to turn him out."

We had almost reached the middle of the garden, which was tucked between two very tall buildings. He let go of my arm and stopped.

"Nice tangerine trees, don't you think?"

I thought they looked rather stunted, they didn't get much sun. But I held my tongue. He went on.

"She has calmed down a bit, about Eugeni. Last year when we went to see Rosamaria, she was nearly out of her mind. She was expecting the boy to turn up at any moment. We could have gone to see them in the winter, when they are in Barcelona, but no, we had to make the trip. She's more resigned now. Sometimes I have the impression that she doesn't think about him much. You haven't heard anything, have you? No, of course you haven't."

I almost told him everything, but the fear in his voice as he posed the question was such that I didn't dare. Later, I thought, when we are back inside.

The garden was narrow and long. The first half was a normal garden; a vegetable patch took up the lower half. The rosebushes were bare and climbed the walls on either side. The earth looked like it had been fertilized.

"We're lucky to have this piece of land. Between what we get from Senyor Maurici, my pension, and the vegetable garden and chickens . . . listen, if you happen to think about it, would you mind sending me some trailing nasturtium seeds, in an envelope?"

I said I didn't have any. I was very sorry but I wouldn't be able to send him any because I had none.

"Yes, you do. By the window of your house. When we were there we saw some trailing nasturtiums."

"You were probably distracted and not paying attention," I said.

"It's true I'm easily distracted, but not always. And I did see the flowers with the little bells, and if I'm not confused in this regard it's because I really like those little blue bells, and next summer I'd like to train them to climb the wall above the henhouse."

"I see what you mean . . . but the trailing nasturtium has yellow flowers, and you're talking about little blue bells. That's why we aren't understanding each other."

He contradicted me. He said he had read in a book that there was a dwarf nasturtium, and that the plant that was called simply nasturtium, without the dwarf part, had yellow flowers, dark yellow flowers, but the nasturtium he was after was the one with the blue bell-shaped flowers, the one railway station masters like to plant, the so-called trailing nasturtium. To avoid arguing about it I said maybe he was right.

"Turn around. See? The apartment next to our house, the one with the veranda with the red and blue stained glass . . . that's where Rosamaria lived with her aunt. Our rooftop terraces touch each other, and Rosamaria used to jump over to ours and come play with Eugeni. Should we head back inside now?"

Senyora Paulina was with a neighbor. As soon as she saw me she said: "You'll stay for lunch, won't you?"

I said I wouldn't be able to because the friend who had driven me would be coming to collect me.

Senyor Andreu pulled me by the arm.

"We'll find a way. Now come see the top of the house."

We went up to the first floor and he showed me around. Then we climbed up to the rooftop terrace.

"See? Just as I said: all along the railing we have flowerpots with ivy geraniums and spiller plants. If I didn't cut them back often they would reach all the way down. On the garden side it's the same."

We leaned over and looked down to the street, and then we looked at the garden. We couldn't lean on the railing because of all the flowerpots.

"Eugeni used to study up here."

He turned the key in the lock and pushed open a sun-bleached, paint-stripped door that moaned on its hinges. We went in. It was a small room, with a sloped ceiling and a small window onto the garden. There was a simple cot, a white wooden table, a chair, and a few empty shelves. A light bulb hung from an electrical wire.

"He liked it up here."

The walls were whitewashed and had patches of dampness. I touched one spot and it left a fine dust on my fingertips.

"It's the rain that does it, of course."

I touched the water-streaked wall again and rubbed my palm against it.

"Don't touch it, better not do that. Nobody would bother him up here. You know, Paulina has always been one to have neighbors over. Especially since I started working at night as a storehouse watchman and slept during the day; she was lonely. This house is open to everyone. Tell me, with all our troubles, what would have become of us without our neighbors?"

We went back out on the rooftop.

"See down there, behind the wall? Yet another new house; they're laying the foundation already. That will be the end of our garden. You should have come before Carrer de Balmes came through here . . . the Riera de Sant Gervasi . . . the narrow path . . . the Marquis de Casa Brusi Forest . . . when we had heavy rains the water swept down the dry riverbed and Eugeni and I would walk over to look at it. Sometimes Rosamaria came too. We would walk there hand in hand, one on either side of me, and we would watch the water raging down."

Suddenly he turned toward me with half-lidded eyes, as if the sunlight was bothering him.

"I'm wondering. Why did you come here?"

"I have something to tell you."

He pretended not to hear me. He walked over to the laundry sinks that were built into the wall adjacent to the room.

"These are the sinks where Paulina bathed the children. Now she says she used to bathe them in a basin, remember? She's losing her memory. This is where she bathed them, in these rooftop sinks, which are the ones we use in winter because the sun warms your back while you're doing the wash. Rosamaria liked to play with clay, making mud pies, they called it, and when they were all grimy from playing Paulina would clean them in the water that had been warmed by the sun and then she would send Rosamaria home, back over the railing . . . would you like to borrow a book or two?"

He showed me back into the room. In a corner there was a trunk. He lifted the cover.

"Some are coming apart. Do any of them strike your fancy? No need to hold on to them forever."

As we were making our way downstairs he said:

"If you're here for the reason I suspect, don't be blunt about it, please. Let her figure it out on her own. The way I have."

"Did you like the house?" said Senyora Paulina wrinkling her nose again. We used to have a nice clear view, but now they're closing in on all sides."

She was standing in the middle of the dining room, as if waiting for us.

"You're staying for lunch. Don't say no, it's decided. What time is the car coming for you?"

I said it would still be a good hour or so.

"If you like, the driver can stay too. You're probably in no hurry."

Senyor Andreu had stopped by the glass door and was looking out into the garden. He appeared despondent.

"You're not going to show him the drawers?" he asked, sounding as if he was making an effort.

"Come, right this way . . . I was waiting for my husband to spare you for a minute."

We entered a dark room. She turned on the light. The bulb gave off a sickly yellow glow and seemed on the point of burning out. I spotted the chest of drawers at once. It had a display case on top, with a Mother of Mercy dressed in a white silk robe embroidered with golden roses and, kneeling at her feet, two slaves in baggy trousers, one in red and the other in purple. One had lost his chain, the other was attached by his to the Virgin's skirt. With considerable effort Senyora Paulina pulled out a drawer. She said the reason it kept getting stuck was that it wasn't level.

"A treasure trove, isn't it?"

The drawer was full of sweaters and socks. She started to close it, and when I was about to help her because I saw she could hardly manage on her own, she slapped my hand down and said if I interfered she would never be able to shut it again. She slid open the drawer beneath it. It too was filled to the brim.

"I knit his socks on the large side," she said, giving a little laugh. "The truth is I can no longer remember what his feet are like."

And just like her husband, with the same words and the same voice, she asked: "Has there been any news of our boy?"

Without giving me a chance to reply, she said: "Andreu says the boy is all right, if he were in trouble he would have written. But I don't believe it."

She was quiet for a moment.

"It's been a while since I saw Senyora Maragda, the seamstress . . . I know she visits there every summer. Those first few years she used to come to see us and we would talk about Eugeni. Then she just disappeared. Everyone grows tired in the end. Why won't the boy write?"

"If he didn't write to you from the beginning, he must have been embarrassed to do so later."

"He could have said something. Anything."

And looking straight at me, her head held high, she said:

"I know I'll never hear from him again."

We went back to the living room. Senyor Andreu was still standing by the glass door looking into the garden. The three of us sat around the table. I thought it was time I told them why I was there. I took the envelope from my pocket and gave it to Senyor Andreu.

"It's for you."

"For us?" she said with a thread of a voice.

Senyor Andreu opened the envelope. His hands were shaking. "Who is it from?"

I said I wasn't free to disclose that information. Senyora Paulina began to weep uncontrollably and we couldn't get another word out of her. Her gaze moved back and forth between him and me. Finally, she said: "Eugeni is dead. As soon as I saw you I was petrified. Rosamaria sends you."

Senyor Andreu fixed his eyes on me.

"Unbelievable. This is no way of doing things. I won't force you to tell me if you have been asked not to . . . but this is not the way to do things."

"It's Rosamaria . . . it's Rosamaria," she kept saying in a stubborn tone.

"If it's Rosamaria then we should thank her."

I don't remember how I managed to convince them not to go see Senyoreta Rosamaria.

"Maybe she doesn't want Francesc to know," said Senyora Paulina, as if stumbling on some half-truth.

I rose and went to take a look at the garden through the window, my back to them.

"He died in an accident. A while ago. Before you came to see the Bohigues family."

I have no idea where all of that was coming from or why I was saying it. But I couldn't stop.

"We only just found out. The person who gave me this for you wants to help. Neither Senyoreta Rosamaria nor Senyoret Francesc know anything about it. You will receive a sum every month. You won't have to struggle to make ends meet anymore."

I turned toward the dining room. They were sitting perfectly still. Her head was bowed and she was moving her lips a little. Senyor Andreu was looking at her but seemed not to see her. No one said anything for some time. Finally I walked over to the table.

"No, no . . . don't leave," Senyora Paulina said as if just waking up. "We said you would stay for lunch. You can't leave us alone now."

She got up and hurried out the door.

"Where are you going?"

"Quiet. Let her be."

She came back with two of her neighbors and they went out into the garden. Senyor Andreu said they were going to get the chicken.

A moment later the doorbell rang. I went to open it; it was Toni, with the car. I told him what was happening and asked him to come back for me midafternoon. He grumbled and said he didn't like to leave the boy alone for so long, not one bit. But he left.

I went back into the living room. Senyor Andreu hadn't budged from his chair. As soon as I appeared he said he was already looking forward to the summer, and to receiving the seeds from me so he would be able to see the swaying of blue nasturtiums blooming above the henhouse. When the neighbors returned with the plucked bird, Senyor Andreu asked if I wanted to go out for an aperitif. I said it wasn't a habit of mine, but this occasion was different. We went to the nearest bar. Senyor Andreu took little sips and was silent. After a while, he set his glass down on the table and he said:

"I think it would be best to buy government bonds." He skewered an olive and examined it from all sides before putting it in his mouth. "Is the yield point four?"

"I don't know."

"If it were point four and a half . . . I'm almost certain it's more than four. Don't you think government bonds are the safest bet?"

He pierced another olive with a toothpick and twirled it around.

"Reminds me of a dancer."

He chewed it slowly.

"I could also sell the house and buy a better one, with more sunlight, but Paulina wouldn't last a week if I made her leave the neighborhood."

He emptied his glass.

"I think the vermouth has gone to my head."

"Same here."

"If we sold the house we would lose our neighbors of course. Who would Paulina talk to about the boy? You know what I'll do with the house? I'll just have it painted for now. In the spring."

He bought two bottles of wine and we went out onto the street. The day was dry and white.

"We'll go up and around through the small square with the trees."

At the square, he stopped.

"See those pepper trees? Eugeni and Rosamaria used to sit under them when they were seeing each other."

When we got back, the table was set and Senyora Paulina asked what had kept us so long. Senyor Andreu still had his mind on the money.

"Government bonds would be best, don't you think, dear?"

"Enriqueta nearly bought some but in the end she decided against it."

When it was time for the chicken, she asked if I preferred the top part or the bottom part. I didn't want to choose, so she gave me a bit of both.

"Have you put the money away?" I asked Senyor Andreu. "We wouldn't want Senyor Maurici to pull one of his tricks."

They looked so crestfallen that I immediately regretted my comment.

When we were having coffee, Senyora Paulina went over to a small desk that stood in a corner near the kitchen door and she brought back a burgundy-colored book with gold lettering. She placed it on the table in front of me.

"It's the book they used to look at together when they were little. Since we told you about it I wanted you to see it."

Then she left and returned with a parcel.

"A few socks. For you."

Then I remembered the knitting needle. Before leaving home I had stuffed it in the inside pocket of my jacket.

"I almost forgot. Here. You must have dropped it on the belvedere."

She took it with great care.

"I think I threw it down. The other one is missing. But thank you for picking it up."

And she began to weep.

When Toni came for me the two of them accompanied me to the door. In the hallway, Senyor Andreu stopped and eased one of the tiles back into place with the tip of his shoe.

"When they were small, Eugeni and Rosamaria used a piece of iron to jimmy it loose. It earned them a good scolding."

They clung to the car door.

"Our regards, our best regards. To everyone. When they come up next summer, please be sure to give them our regards."

When we reached the corner I turned to look at them through the rear window. They had already gone back inside.

Senyor Bellom was waiting for us. I told him everything was taken care of.

"One less thing . . . Now my daughter says she wants to go to California. I told her to do whatever she wants. I would rather have her here, but if she's going to be miserable . . ."

He bit his lip.

"Did you talk much about Eugeni?"

I told him everything, beginning to end. When I had finished, he rose.

"You might not believe this, but when I saw you setting off with Toni this morning, a sort of calm came over me . . . you know what had been on my mind constantly? Eugeni's smashed face. It kept me awake at night."

VI

THAT WAS THE LAST SUMMER. An unpleasant summer of rain-filled days. From one moment to the next we went from hot to cold and from cold to hot. One night toward the end of June, I had to put on the sweater Eugeni had given me.

They arrived after the summer solstice of the Feast of Saint John. I heard Senyoreta Rosamaria had scarcely left the flat all winter. The spring weather had lightened her spirits, but she was still complaining of fatigue. Things were going well for Senyoreta Eulàlia. The exhibit in New York had earned her some money, and when it was time to return she bought herself a cherry-red automobile. Feliu had a show in Barcelona, but no one talked about it. According to Quima, Senyoreta Maragda and Senyoreta Rosamaria were considering going into business together, setting up a big fashion house. But it was only talk.

I ran into Mariona on the street the day she arrived. I was returning from paying a visit to Bergadans, who had been taken ill, and she was out shopping for espadrilles. She was walking ahead of me and I caught up with her.

"So, I'm guessing Mingo has decamped."

"Far from it! We're getting married the first Sunday in August."

"What would you like as a gift?"

She stopped and thought for a moment, and she must have had trouble coming up with something because she said I should give her whatever I wanted to. When we reached the gate I asked her if she was planning to quit work.

"Not for now. Mingo and I talked about it and we decided I would continue until a baby comes."

"Don't be in a hurry, only headaches after that."

She laughed and leaned against the gate. She seemed in no hurry to go inside.

"What do you think of Mingo?"

"What do you mean?"

"I mean do you think he's a good man."

"Well . . ."

"Everyone says the same: well . . ."

"My dear, can't you see you are practically married now? You should have asked me this a long time ago."

She laughed again.

"My mind is made up. I'm just asking because I like to know what people think."

"I see you no longer say, 'My foot!'"

"No. Mingo doesn't like it. He says I sound like a country girl."

Suddenly she remembered that Miranda was waiting for her to polish the silver and she left me standing there. I walked across the garden very slowly, gazing up at the trees and the branches outlined against the sky.

Senyor Bellom rarely showed his face. He had been away for quite a while, and when he was at the house he shut himself indoors. One day Quima said to me:

"It seems he's no longer drinking himself silly. At least not at Can Bergadans." It pained me to talk about it, so I didn't reply. She acted like she was distracted, and she said: "Senyoreta Rosamaria has yet to set foot on the beach . . . you must have noticed."

I couldn't shake Quima off. Another day she told me that Maribel was in America and wrote to her father every week. I knew as much from the postman. I said I wasn't interested in hearing about these things. She turned beet red.

"You sure have changed, haven't you? You must be getting old; you don't seem to find joy in anything anymore."

I thought maybe she was right.

Despite the bad weather, my summer roses were the loveliest they had ever been. Then a heavy rain left them half dead. To help pass the time I planted a ring of flowers near the gate, with one layer of cineraria and another of Peruvian vanilla, and I filled the center with fiery-red begonias. Whenever I had to work for a long stretch without stopping I would take my transistor with me and listen to the radio.

The first person to notice was Quima.

"You even have a radio." She picked it up and inspected it from all angles.

"It was given to me."

"The masters?"

I took a while to reply because I didn't want her to know. But in the end I told her.

"Eugeni."

She shook her head for a moment and was silent.

"Poor Eugeni. No one remembers him anymore."

"Is that so?"

"A few visits from Maribel to the cemetery and then it was over."

She started to leave but then she turned around.

"Believe me, no one remembers Eugeni. And even if they did, what does it matter?"

One day I decided to tidy up the honeysuckle, which was overgrown and trailing too much. I was busy all morning. I planted reed stalks to hold up the plants, making an effort to keep them out of sight. It looked nice. As I was finishing up, I spotted Feliu and Senyoreta Eulàlia making their way to the beach along the path to the greenhouse. They stopped to shake my hand and were very kind to me. She seemed cheerful, and there was a happy glint in her eyes.

"I understand your exhibit was a success."

"She sold every last piece, and then she was sad because she sold some she wished she had kept," Feliu said.

"What about the Saint Joseph with crusted eyes?" I said.

"It was the first to go."

When I no longer knew what to talk about, I remembered something Feliu had mentioned the previous year.

"Tell me, did you get around to painting that five-meter canvas?"

He looked surprised, as if he didn't know what I was referring to.

"A five-meter painting?"

I thought, "Maybe you only dreamed it," but his memory must have caught up with him all of a sudden because he gave a little rabbit laugh.

"Goodness, what a keen memory! I'd better watch what I say to you." And he kicked a stone.

I'm sure I wouldn't have given that conversation another thought, had it not been for the fact that, as they were leaving, Feliu said to me: "Whatever you do, don't let Miranda out of your sight. Please."

Mariona's wedding was quite lavish. The inside of the village church gleamed and was filled to the brim. Senyoreta Rosamaria rose before the Mass was over and left. She said she was indisposed. Senyoret Francesc didn't move. Miranda wept the entire time. After the service, Senyoreta Eulàlia's eyes were red. I still don't understand why. I thought it was all rather funny.

Mariona came back fifteen days after the wedding. She said Mingo was working in Esplugues, and she had already spoken to the masters and had agreed not to leave them in the middle of the season. Quima was upset. She had always liked Mariona, but she could barely tolerate her since she returned from her honeymoon.

Toni was the one who kept talking to me about her. We had attended the wedding together. One evening he came to the house for coffee. Now that he had his son with him, he no longer stopped by as often.

"A girl like Mariona would have been good for me. And I had her right here all these summers. But she was too young for me, don't you think?"

He was angry at his son and growing angrier by the day. The boy had run away a few times, but he always came back three or four days later, dirty as a pig, hungry as a wolf.

"If only he would stay gone! He could go off to America and make it rich like Senyor Bellom."

The boy was no longer helping him with the horses. At the beginning of the summer some folks from Barcelona had come up and taken Senyor Bellom's horses away. There had been no news of them since. As he had been paid handsomely by Senyor Bellom until then, this only worsened Toni's ill humor.

The following morning, I was leaving the house and I noticed he was taking Lucifer out of the stable. When he saw me he called to me.

"I haven't slept a wink. I'm at a loss."

I recalled the day he had arrived with the horses. Short and arrogant.

"I'm wasting my money on that fool. What would you do? Maybe I should have him apprenticed somewhere. But if I send him down to Barcelona to learn a trade, where will he live? My cousin won't have him. And why would she? And here in the village they won't even hire him to pull up onions . . ."

"Why not keep him as a stable boy?"

"One in a family is quite enough. Too much, even."

"Give it a year. Maybe he'll come around."

"It's not easy. He takes after his maternal grandfather. Not much hope there."

He began to brush Lucifer, who had grown really tame, and you wouldn't believe the dust he whisked up.

That summer never got off the ground. Everything seemed to be at a standstill. And the weather continued to be erratic. In late August it began to rain nonstop. Fifteen days it lasted. The earth struggled to swallow all the water, and I was afraid my entire garden would rot. They locked themselves indoors. Perhaps in an attempt to dispel the general gloom, Feliu went down to Barcelona one day to collect a friend of his who made films. And it was like the friend brought good luck with him, because the following day the rain stopped. He was a fellow of about thirty, short, a little bald in the back, with blue eyes that bulged and jerked.

His name was Humbert and he never stopped smoking. He spent two or three quiet days strolling along the beach and taking photographs of the garden. And according to Quima, he started running after Miranda right away.

"Now she's playing the saint. What do you think of that? Yesterday I heard her telling him that if he didn't leave her alone she was going to tell the masters. That old woman was right . . ."

When he had mulled things over to his satisfaction, Humbert began his preparations. First he had me move quite a few flowerpots. They didn't look right, he said. Then he gave us all a lengthy explanation of what we were to do. The weather was nice, and Feliu said it would be better to take advantage of it and get started at once, without quite so much speechifying. We pretended the masters were having their breakfast under the magnolia trees and the girls were serving. Miranda immediately got it right but Mariona struggled. She couldn't get it out of her head that she was being filmed, and she came on the scene with her back stiff as a board. Humbert had a good laugh at her expense, but he grew more and more exasperated.

"This girl is a bit thick," he said when he had made her walk up and down half a dozen times.

He didn't make me lose my patience because I have plenty of it. My job was to crouch above a thicket of flame pansies pretending to work. "It shouldn't be difficult for you," he said. "It's probably all you do." And he gave an asinine laugh. It really bothered me that a layabout like him would talk to me that way, but I thought I had better keep the peace. He said my movements should be natural and not exaggerated for effect. But he was never pleased with what I did. I was turning sideways too much. I was bending down too fast. Just as I was about to walk off and leave him stranded it began to rain again and we had to call off the whole thing.

In the evening I went out in my hooded rain slicker. They were all standing by the main door to the house, under the awning, looking grim and gazing up at the sky saying maybe tomorrow, maybe the day after that.

Quima wasn't in the film and she was very upset about it.

"The only people they invite up here are fools who create a lot of work for the rest of us. This nobody has them all in his pocket. He dresses like a tramp. And you know how he sleeps? The wrong way around. With his head at the foot of the bed. Mariona, who does his room, couldn't help but ask him why he sleeps like that. Every morning she finds the pillow and upper end of the bedsheet at the footboard. He said he doesn't get a wink of sleep if his head is on the side where the sun rises. Ever heard of such a thing? And he eats like a horse. He always has his breakfast in bed, four fried eggs that we have to send up to him."

It rained for a couple of days, and when it stopped they filmed the part with the horses. Toni was supposed to introduce himself to Senyoreta Rosamaria while leading Fletxa by a rope. The first time around we all had a good laugh because Toni, who wasn't too keen on the whole thing, had tied the horse with a very long rope and it looked like we were making some kind of comedy. I was sitting at a distance, on an upturned flowerpot, and when Fletxa spotted me he slowly turned around, plodded over to me, and started bobbing his head.

Humbert came close to having a nervous attack that day. In the end they got what they were after, more or less, and they spent the afternoon on the linden promenade photographing the ladies on their horses.

The following day they went to the beach and filmed by themselves.

The first piece of bad news arrived a week later. I had already had my dinner when Toni showed up.

"I'm leaving."

"You?"

"They're letting me go."

"Whatever for?"

"They're selling the horses. They even asked me if I would arrange it, place a few advertisements in the papers or write to some of my acquaintances about it . . ."

"That's all?"

"It's quite enough, don't you think? They're giving me three months' pay, and go find yourself another job. If you thought they were going to be gentlemanly about it . . ."

"Fletxa, too?"

"Didn't I say they're selling the horses? Yes, both of them."

I was rattled, and I spent the night ruminating on it. The following day, when Humbert said he wanted to take my picture, I said I wasn't feeling well. After lunch I went to see Quima.

"What are you doing here?"

As always, there was the vase with the parsley, the white transistor radio, and that wonderful smell of stew.

"He's probably lonely," Mariona said. "I don't understand how he can live like that, surrounded by seeds and bulbs."

They gave me a cup of coffee and we talked for a good while. I stopped by a few days in a row. On the last day, when I saw that Quima wasn't going to tell me anything, I said: "Did you know they were selling the horses?"

She was drying a beautiful piece of silver, as if she was its custodian, and she nearly dropped it. She reacted the way I did: the first thing she asked was if they would keep Senyoreta's horse.

"They're not keeping either of them. They've already given Toni his notice."

"I wouldn't mind at all if they were to let me go," Quima said. "I only come here and cook for them in the summer as a favor. I'd be more comfortable in my own home. My kitchen doesn't have raised windows like these, it's on the ground level and looks onto a courtyard."

Misfortunes never come alone, and Toni's boy ran away again and came back with his head all smashed.

Three or four men stopped by to see the horses. Toni accompanied them to the stable, took a little pad from his pocket, and read them his notes. They looked the horses up and down, asked a few questions, scratched their heads, and went away undecided. But one day someone did come who knew just what he was after: a horse for his son. And he took Lucifer. The very next day they came for him with a truck, and the animal was so panicked that they struggled to get him inside. A friend of Toni's kept Fletxa. Before the horses were removed, Humbert took pictures of them, and I asked him for copies of both, as keepsakes. I asked how much I owed him but he refused to charge me.

One evening when Toni and I were chatting at the foot of the eucalyptus, his son walked by with his head bandaged.

"What a sight," he said. "I still haven't been able to figure out what happened to him."

He laughed half-heartedly. I asked him when he was leaving.

"I'll stay on a few more days. Next week I want to go down to Barcelona to look for an apartment."

"What about the furniture?"

"I've put everything in storage; it's costing me an arm and a leg. Lousy business, my time here."

"It's already a lot, if you have furniture . . ."

I said it in good faith, but he was put out.

Humbert was busy photographing the sea, the foam bubbling atop the waves, and everything he could find on the sand. The wasted hours he squandered away. One morning he walked the cliff-side path and took pictures of the pine trees that grew above the rocks.

The nights were calm. Sometimes a kind of anguish would drive me outdoors, but nothing was astir. In the garden something had changed but I couldn't explain exactly what it was. I was starting to feel old. There were plants I should have already replaced, but I must have lacked the energy. I would say to myself: You'll do it tomorrow. But it was never the right moment. Mostly I wanted to stop thinking. I wanted to listen instead to the rustling of the leaves and, even more, to the sound of the rain on the roof as I was falling asleep. As for the family, once the excitement of the filming and photographing was over, they didn't appear overly downcast; it was more like they weren't even there. When I strolled past the belvedere I often thought of Senyoret Sebastià and how we had laughed the night we went around taking everyone's picture while they slept. There was joy then. Poor Humbert, who turned out to be a better person than he seemed at first, was like an undertaker compared to Sebastià. It was plain that all of that could not last.

Around that time Mariona came to see me.

"I miss Mingo. I don't want to live like this anymore. One day he's going to fall off the scaffolding and by the time the news reaches me he'll be dead."

She said Senyoreta Rosamaria and Senyoreta Maragda had had a terrible row. I asked what had happened.

"I'm not sure. Miranda's the one who knows the story, but she's acting strange these days, she wouldn't tell me a thing. Senyoreta

Maragda has already left. Senyoreta Eulàlia drove her to Barcelona in her car this morning. We probably won't see any more of her."

I had never been close to Senyoreta Maragda. I don't think I ever had a conversation with her. But I was sorry she had left.

That night Mariona came back.

I could tell something was wrong as soon as I saw her. She stood in the middle of the dining room, she walked over to the window, she peered outside . . . if she had done this good a job of acting on the day they did the filming, Humbert would have been very pleased.

"What are you doing out at this hour?"

She sat down at the table.

"I know it's late, but if I hadn't come to see you I wouldn't have been able to sleep."

"Has something happened to Mingo?"

Rather than reply, she said: "This afternoon I was doing Senyoreta Maragda's room. I hadn't cleaned it earlier because she's already gone, so it wasn't urgent. I found this notebook in the drawer of her bedside table."

She removed from her apron pocket a small, thick notebook with black oilcloth covers.

"I didn't mean to, but I read part of it. I feel really bad about it."

I thought it best to get on with it.

"Look Mariona, it's late and I'm tired. Why don't you stop by tomorrow, in the daytime, and you can tell me all about it?"

She stood up, but sat back down immediately.

"No. I can't leave. I would have told Quima, but she's barely spoken to me since I've been back. And it's none of Miranda's business. That's why I've come to you. I've always had a warm feeling for you, and I think you feel the same way about me."

"If you don't explain yourself . . ."

"I don't know where to begin."

It wasn't easy but finally she told me. The notebook was mostly about Senyoreta Rosamaria, and she was sure it had belonged to Eugeni.

"I don't know what to do. I can't very well hand it over to Senyoreta Rosamaria. And I'd be embarrassed to keep it and return it to Senyoreta Maragda when I go back to Barcelona. She'll think I've read it. What should I do?"

I held out my hand and she gave it to me.

"You know Eugeni's parents . . . maybe it would be best for them to have it."

"Maybe . . ."

I opened the notebook. Eugeni had written down everything that happened to him. The first section I read dealt with the fight he'd had with Francesc on the street. I skipped ahead. He talked about how he had fallen in love, very slowly and over a period of time. On summer evenings they would meet on Carrer d'Elisa, they walked hand in hand to the little square and sat beneath the pepper trees. When they were fourteen, if two or three days went by without seeing each other, she would go to his house for some flowers. If she was asked to stay for lunch, he would become transfixed just looking at her. He helped her with her lessons and her math homework. She searched the school grounds for four-leaf clovers and would slip them between the pages of his history book when she went to his house to study.

He talked a lot about a dress she had worn one summer. And

suddenly I remembered my Cecília's dresses. The color of rosemary flowers. There were few similarities, but still it seemed to me they had loved each other the way we had loved each other, me and Cecília. One day when it rained a lot, he spent the night listening to the water gushing down the dry riverbed; the following day she told him she had thought about him all night. Farther along he began to write about Francesc, and it seems they both made fun of him. She didn't like him because he was rich and pretentious. And poor Eugeni wrote in his notebook that she was becoming pretty as an angel.

Mariona stood and looked out the window.

"Isn't it rather late for you?"

She said it wasn't and sat back down. I read on. I skipped entire pages because I wanted to come to the end. I thought about Cecília, so young when I lost her.

One day Rosamaria started to be afraid. She had just turned eighteen. She was terrified she would be forced to sew her entire life, until the day she died. She told Eugeni this when she visited him in his room on the rooftop. They spent hours kissing in bed, growing sadder and sadder. One summer night when he wasn't expecting her, she spilled her heart out to him. She said she had meant to tell him why sometimes she went out for a stroll with Francesc. She said she loved only him, she and Francesc were just friends, and she began to kiss him. They stayed there all night; at dawn, when he was alone again, he was filled with sadness. For a long time they were racked with fear, scarcely living, afraid their one night together had sufficed to leave her with child. It all came to nothing; she was late because she had bathed on the days she was indisposed. When the fear passed, she turned to Francesc, quietly . . . until the neighbors found out, and by the time the neighbors found out things were well advanced. They had grown attached. Eugeni nearly went mad, and there was nothing he could do about it.

I closed the notebook and left it on the table.

Mariona asked: "Why would Senyoreta Maragda have it?"

I remembered Senyora Paulina telling me that Senyoreta Maragda often went to keep them company after Eugeni left home. Maybe Senyora Paulina gave her the notebook one day and never thought about it again. What I couldn't understand was why Senyoreta Maragda would leave it in her bedside table. But perhaps it was best not to understand.

"What do you think I should do?" Mariona said. "Senyoreta Maragda and Senyoreta Rosamaria don't like each other at all. I know because I used to go to Senyoreta Maragda's house to learn to sew, and one of the girls who worked there mentioned that their mistress had wanted to marry Senyoret Francesc."

I studied her for a while. She was white as a sheet and her eyes were filled with fear.

"Don't worry. We'll fix this right now."

I went outside, and slowly I ripped the pages from the notebook. When I had them all crumpled on the ground, I set them on fire. Mariona watched from the doorway.

I thought the burnt oilcloth would cause a stench, so I tore it up and tossed it behind the honeysuckle.

On Sunday when she brought the laundry, Quima could barely utter a word. I thought she might be ill. Her face was red and she was short of breath, as if she had been running.

"Senyor Bellom is getting married!"

A vein in her neck was bulging, and I feared it might burst and she would fall dead at my feet. I didn't know what to do.

"Sit down and catch your breath."

I was starting to grow weary of so much nonsense. I thought that if Senyor Bellom wanted to marry he was free to do so, and there shouldn't be such a fuss. I said as much. But when she was finally able to tell me that Senyor Bellom was marrying Miranda, I was speechless.

"And how do you know?"

"I just found out from Bergadans."

"What does Bergadans have to do with it?"

She said Bergadans knew all about it because Senyor Bellom had been seeing Miranda for some time and they had spent many afternoons together at the inn.

"Bergadans is building himself a little house outside the village and everyone knows where he got the money for it."

Then, as if suddenly unhinged, she let out a laugh that must have been heard as far as in the village.

"Miranda! What do you say to that? Apparently Senyor Bellom likes them with a nice tan."

I was reminded of Lilit, but I didn't say anything. She wouldn't drop it.

"At first I almost fell over, but now I'm just amused."

She said the house was empty because the masters and Humbert were traipsing through the cemetery taking pictures of the crosses. After Quima left, I was so eager to talk about it that I didn't stop until I tracked down Toni. When he learned the news he wasn't impressed.

"You ask me, I have nothing against Miranda. I'm glad she's been lucky."

That same day, Miranda, carrying a large suitcase, moved in with Senyor Bellom. I would have given anything to see the look on the masters' faces as they said goodbye. She left proud as a peacock, Mariona said.

"At least someone will be enjoying themselves. Senyor Bellom has promised to take her to Brazil and parade her up and down the country like a queen."

A few days later they both came by to see me. I was standing near the hedgerow and I told them to come to the house. She didn't open her mouth, she spent the entire time looking at the sunflowers on the wall. He admitted he was aware that the news of his marriage had come as a shock, but he didn't care. He had reached a point in his life where he wanted to think of himself.

"If I don't look out for my own interests, no one else will."

He asked me to attend the wedding. I didn't want to, but he insisted, and I finally said I would go. I told Miranda that if Senyoret Francesc allowed me to pick a few white flowers I would make the bouquet for her. She seemed pleased.

They married with great pomp. The masters were there, looking as if they had just been lifted out of a box. Miranda dressed in white. She carried my bouquet of tuberoses, heavy flowers of course, but I thought she was used to a lack of refinement and wouldn't mind a little weight. A shiny silk dress, a long train, a lace veil. The party was like the ones they used to host in previous summers, but with fewer people. And I was able to see her up close.

When Mariona, who was also invited, saw the amount of work the reception entailed, the poor girl couldn't restrain herself and immediately went about serving the guests. The dance lasted until dawn. The masters left early. I lingered because I didn't want to leave Mariona alone. Finally I told her I thought it was time to go, and she took my advice. As we were making our way back she said to me: "I wonder what Mingo is doing now. Aren't we a couple of fools, living separate lives?"

They left on their honeymoon and the house was like a cemetery. Josep strolled back and forth among the cypress trees with the book on flowers, absorbed in his reading.

I accompanied Toni to the station. He had found an apartment in Barcelona. A man who died of old age had lived there before. Toni said that even if he found a job elsewhere he would still keep the apartment because the fear of not finding one had almost been too much for him. His son was trailing behind us at a good distance, as if he didn't know us. We were plodding along, discussing the wedding, and when we were in front of the station and I was about to hold out my hand to shake his goodbye, he said: "You know what I'll remember the most? That summer with the monkey. Such a tedious time, wasn't it?"

And he headed inside. I watched as he walked away with a suitcase in each hand, and by Jove the man was short.

I had to pass by Can Bergadans on my way home, so I went in to say hello. He pulled out a postcard he had just received from Senyor Bellom: it showed a very wide river. I had a glass of anisette because I felt a tightness in my chest, and then I left. On the way back I thought about what Toni had said; a scant hour earlier, as I was waiting to accompany him to the station, I had noticed there were still traces of color on the trunks of the pittosporums from when Tití had smeared paint on them.

A few days later Senyoret showed up in his Sunday best.

"I'm just stopping for a moment," he said. "I'm going to Barcelona for a week. I wanted to tell you that I've decided to sell the house."

He said he had not forgotten about me and would be paying me a full year's wages from the date of their departure, in late September. Several announcements had already been published, and if that didn't bear fruit he would put an agent in charge of the sale, but he preferred to sell the house directly, through advertising, because that would allow him to give me three percent of the money from the sale. He brought out a pen, made his calculations, and said: "See? With a direct sale you'll get this amount."

It was a tidy sum. I thanked him for his kindness, but I didn't have the heart to see him to the door, for not only would I be left high and dry, but the truth is I was fond of them.

Mariona said to me: "We leave tomorrow."

Senyoret Francesc had already explained that someone would be coming for the furniture while they were away and had asked me to take care of everything. It was late, and it was drizzling. A light rain of the kind that falls between summer and autumn, when the air is filled with the cessation of being: a fine drizzle, barely a mist. At midnight I still had not been able to sleep, so I went out. I wandered toward the linden promenade, one hand in my pocket, rubbing the coin with the crescent moon between my fingers. I glimpsed a weightless shadow walking soundlessly, threading her way through the linden trees, barefoot. When she reached the belvedere she paused for a moment, draped a white towel over the railing, and went down to the beach. I hurried to see what she was doing. She stood facing the sea, so still she seemed immaterial. The clouds had thinned, and a sliver of moon came probing through. She turned around and I concealed myself behind a flowerpot, just as I had on that night with Senyoret Francesc and Miranda. The rain continued to fall. She stood on the sand like a salt statue. Just as I was beginning to tire, she slowly waded into the water and began to swim. I couldn't say whether she swam far out or stayed near the shore, for suddenly everything darkened and I could see very little, only the inky sweep, with the coming and going of the waves. Onward, onward, onward . . . we come and we go . . . and a strange thought occurred to me: that she was on her way to meet Eugeni at the place where he had willed himself to die. To say goodbye to him, as it were. I stood listening to the great exhalations of the water until at last I saw her emerge and let herself drop to the ground, exhausted. A moment later I heard someone behind me. It was Senyoret Francesc; he put a finger to his lips to signal for me to be silent, and I moved aside. She climbed the stairs to the belvedere and he bundled her up. "Don't you see you'll come down with something?" He took her in his arms and put his cheek to hers. I heard him say: "You can't go around with your face so cold, now can you?" And they left like that, heading up toward the trees. I stayed to listen to the sea, and I could almost hear him say: "Saving seeds? . . . I used to remove the kernels from wallflowers myself . . . Can I give you a hand?"

Senyoreta Eulàlia and Feliu left early the next morning, with Mariona. All three of them in the red car. They were in fine spirits. They said they would come to see me and would send me postcards, and if by chance they went abroad, I would receive postcards from abroad.

The masters left midafternoon. Quima and I were the only ones left. We waited for them by the gate. I had put together a bouquet of flowers for Senyoreta, so large it nearly engulfed her. They put it inside the car. Then Senyoreta reached out her hand, and just as I was about to shake it I realized I still had the coin in my hand.

"Oh. Excuse me," I said. And I slipped it back in my pocket.

"May I?"

"It's nothing . . . they say it brings good luck."

I almost asked if she wanted to have it, but something held me back. They climbed in the car and we stood at the gate until they turned the corner.

Senyor Bellom and Miranda were soon back from their honeymoon. Some fifteen days later, as the masters' furniture was being removed, Josep came to see me and said that Senyor Bellom wished to speak to me.

He sat facing the windows, in one of those large armchairs, very calm. He might have been a little thinner.

"I hear the Bohigues family are selling the house. What's your situation? I mean what are your means, how will you get by?"

I explained it all exactly as it was.

"Well . . . I get a year's wages, and if they sell the house directly, three percent of the selling price. Quima said if the new owners don't want to keep me on, she'll have me at her place for free, on the condition that I look after her vegetable garden. I would pay for my own food of course."

He studied me calmly, stretched his legs, and said:

"If that's the case . . . but if you need anything . . . I could always find some kind of job for you here, whatever you feel up to. Small things: sorting seeds, arranging the bulbs . . . and if that's too much, you can forget it and just come to see me every year around Christmas, and wish me a happy holiday. I've always liked it when people wish me a Merry Christmas. Fair enough?"

Later we talked about many other things. Brazil and the plants they grow there, a hotel in Rio where you sit outside to have your meal and flocks of flamingoes—pink birds, peaceful things—come to watch you . . . beaches that never end.

We stood up and wandered outside. Slowly we started walking toward the boxwood hedge. The grass between the flat pebbles was the color of straw.

"When these cypress trees are tall, you and I will have been beneath the earth for many years."

"Senyor Bellom, I don't know how to thank you . . ."

He raised a hand and halted my words with his gesture.

"Look at the sea, what a smooth back it has . . ."

"I must thank you but you won't let me. You know what? If I'm forced to leave this place, it will be my death. Maybe whoever buys the house will keep me on, like Senyoret Francesc did. I'll tell this person that I work like a young man . . . only with more experience. You know the whole story, and you know that my Cecília died. Such is life. But while I'm here she won't be gone, not completely . . . believe me, it's true: she won't be completely dead. I've lived here since I was a soldier, here in this house, as you know. Day in day out . . . look at the garden now, this is the best hour, the best time to sense its vigor and capture its scent. Look at the linden trees. See the leaves, how they tremble and listen to us. You laugh now, but one day if you find yourself walking in the garden at night, beneath the trees, you will see how the garden talks to you, the things it says . . ."

We parted there, by the belvedere, and it was, as they say, the end of the story.

Geneva, September 1-17, 1959 – December, 1966.

MERCÈ RODOREDA is widely regarded as the most important Catalan writer of the twentieth century. Exiled in France and Switzerland following the Spanish Civil War, Rodoreda began writing the novels and short stories that would eventually make her internationally famous, while at the same time earning a living as a seamstress.

The mother and daughter translation team of MARTHA TENNENT and MARUXA RELAÑO has translated a number of works from Spanish and Catalan into English, including *War, So Much War* by Mercè Rodoreda. Tennent also received an NEA fellowship for her translation of *The Selected Stories of Mercè Rodoreda*.

**OPEN
LETTER**

**OPEN
LETTER**